THE
MOSSAD
WARRIOR SPY

Mark Cohn Series, Book 3

MARK AKST

Canoe Tree
Press

**Previous Novels
in the Mark Cohn Series
By Mark Akst**

.~୭୨ଏ~.

King Herod's Treasure

Mark Cohn and the Secrets of the Saffron Mountain

TABLE OF CONTENTS

CHAPTER ONE

THE HERO

It was a hidden jungle tree root. No higher than three inches, jutting above the ground and covered with rotting dead leaves that caused the accident. Major Eric Jansen, running hard in full battle gear, his eyes fixed on the fleeing enemy terrorists, simply did not see the disguised root. The tip of his boot got caught on it, causing him to trip. Down he went, hitting his head hard on a huge, low growing tree branch, knocking him out cold. The last thing he remembered was his nostrils filled with the still half damp, rancid smell of "forest" elephant dung on the jungle floor before he passed out. Even the best trained warriors can have an accident. His superb tracking skills as a hunter had brought his troop this far. At the moment, though, bad for him but fortuitous for the troop of Sayeret Matkal (Israeli Special Forces equivalent to US Navy SEALs), in which he was attached from the Mossad, Israel's lethal spy agency. His fellow commandos saw him fall. Not knowing what had caused it, they spread out further, stopping their pursuit to take cover in the lush jungle growth of Central Africa. Their quick reaction avoided the machine gun ambush the fleeing terrorists had set up around the next bend. By spreading out, the Israelis forced the terrorists to come to them instead, saving the commandos' lives. A ferocious gun battle ensued. All of which took place over the body of Eric Jansen lying flat, knocked senseless, on the ground. Moreover, the blistering machine gun crossfire from the terrorists was so intense that the Israeli commandos, with much cursing and regret but with no other choice, had to begrudgingly withdraw, leaving their comrade and friend, Major Eric Jansen, behind. Afterwards, they swore they would not rest until they got him back.

This military operation was put together so quickly when the bus load of Israeli tourists in Egypt had been kidnapped by as yet unknown terrorists. The bus had been driven to a makeshift airport in southern Egypt where the women and children hostages had been split off from a dozen Israeli men, who had been taken aboard a plane. The male hostages were then flown to the Central African Republic, a nation mostly covered in dense jungle and in constant civil war. Eric Jansen was perfect for the rescue mission. He was both a Mossad and Special Forces trained operative who spoke numerous languages. When his military contact had told him about this secret mission to rescue the hostages, he had volunteered instantly. His reserve status was now active again. Moreover, he secretively relished the idea of another life or death terrorist hunt.

He had just one not-so-small problem. He had promised Mark Cohn, his married partner of more than three years, that he had retired from the Mossad and all the dangerous missions that came along with it. However, the reality was that Eric continued to use his reputation as a famous archeologist to book speaking engagements in different countries as a cover for his Mossad assignments. Mark had accompanied him at first on these trips but soon grew bored with Eric's lecture tours. So now Eric always traveled alone. Besides, Mark was basically a homebody while Eric definitely was not. In fact, there was a part of Eric that thrived on the animal energy of the hunt and yes, the killing too. His partner had sensed this part of Eric and called it his "black side." But when they were together, Eric kept this part of himself carefully tucked away and hidden from view. This time he told Mark that he would be in Cairo for a few days for a last minute lecture and some research, then return home—nothing exciting. Eric didn't like lying to Mark but wanted to save Mark the pain and stress of worrying about him.

Eric awoke two days later, his six foot, two inch naked body chained face down on a stone table with a headache and bump on his forehead. He immediately started taking stock of where he was and what had happened to him. His wrists wore ancient iron handcuffs stretching the top half of his hard muscled body across the stone slab. The chains were attached to stone walls about five feet away. The bottom half of his body was bent over the edge of the stone table with his two feet spread apart chained to the floor. There was a small square hole cut high up into one of the walls letting air and light stream into the room. He recognized the antique iron handcuffs as the kind worn by slaves in the nineteenth century. He had to be careful not to jerk his hands too much because the sharp edges of his handcuffs could cut into his wrists, making his flesh bleed. The air was hot, humid, and smelled of jungle foliage, which Eric recognized. He guessed this was one of the places the old time slavers had kept their slaves on the way to be sold. He could also hear rushing water from what seemed like a large river. From this, Eric continued to guess he was being kept on one of the ancient slave trading routes near the White Nile head waters. It then also dawned on him that he was completely naked. All his state of the art military gear, uniform, boots, and underwear had been stripped off. The room was dead silent except when he heard a man yelling in Hebrew from the next room for water. He knew he had found the hostages as he thought, *Now to escape!* But he didn't have time to act.

Two minutes later, behind him and out of sight, Eric heard an old wooden door to his room swing open and close. In walked the commander and two younger bodyguards in dirty and worn uniforms carrying machine guns. The commander of the kidnappers was a huge, mean-looking African, about forty years old, who stood six foot, four inches tall and weighed more than 250 pounds, most of it muscle. He also was, as Eric was about to discover, what half of Africa already knew, a born sadist. His two younger African bodyguards were about the same height with tightly muscled bodies. The commander politely introduced himself in Arabic using a dialect Eric knew was common in northern Nigeria. The commander's name was Mohammed Al Kaduna. He also mentioned that more of his army would be arriving soon, but for the moment they were all alone. Eric felt certain this group was an offshoot of Boko Haram, the fanatical Islamist terrorist organization based in northern Nigeria that had kidnapped those young Christian school girls several years ago, raped them, then forced them to marry and convert to Islam.

Next, the commander did something that Eric thought odd. He grabbed, almost caressing, Eric's ass as he walked around the table so Eric could clearly see him. The instant the commander did this, Eric knew he was going to be raped and murdered. Otherwise, the commander would never have allowed Eric to see his face or know his name. He was also a little surprised when the commander knew his name. Eric knew that he could not have discovered it from his military gear since no identification was allowed on such missions. But the mystery was solved when the commander announced he was an amateur archeologist and recognized Eric from his televised lectures. He switched to broken English from Arabic when he said, "I am a fan of your lectures about your archeological expeditions where you made such big discoveries of ancient gold and treasure." Moreover, as his lecherous eyes stared at Eric's prostrated body, he added, "And I always thought you were a truly handsome man, even too pretty for a man." At this point he ran his fingers through Eric's yellow-blond hair. When he did this, the two bodyguards chuckled nervously as if they anticipated what was about to happen. The commander then proceeded to light a cigar as he ran his big, sweaty hand along Eric's naked spine. Eric's body involuntarily tensed in repulsion, arching his back and forcing up into the air his two white, melon-shaped buns, exactly the physical response the commander wanted. At the same time, Eric unintentionally pulled on his iron handcuffs, causing the edges of the cuffs to painfully cut into his wrists and bleed. The sight of Eric's blood, helplessness, and perfect buns in a penetration position heightened the sexual interest of his three torturers. Surprisingly to Eric, the commander then burned the lighted tip of his cigar into one of Eric's exposed, milky white butt cheeks. This caused Eric to scream in pain. Switching into Arabic, which Eric understood perfectly, and laughing, the commander announced, "You are going to make another very big discovery today. But this time, about the men in this part of Africa!" Then with a nod from the commander, one of the bodyguards unzipped his pants and began to savagely rape Eric. He felt something deep in him give way and dissolve while he screamed in pain with something that huge forced inside him. Now, however, it was a deep guttural scream. Concurrently, the more Eric pulled on his handcuffs, the deeper the edges cut and the more blood and now sweat poured from his wrists and hands. Eric's body was sweating profusely from being so sexually and painfully violated. Finally, the first bodyguard finished, laughing all the way. The second man now unzipped his pants to take his turn. The commander sneered at Eric, saying, "The first guy was just the warmup for you! After the next one, you will be ready for me. And I'll show you what big really is!" Strangely, hearing this comment, Eric was not scared but disgusted with himself for allowing himself to be put in this position, while at the same time a steely resolve overwhelmed him to survive.

During the minute or so that it took for the second man to position himself behind Eric, he noticed that one of the guards had laid his machine gun on the table next to his prostrated, naked body. He could feel the outline of gun metal touching the side of his flesh. Eric thought the guard did this to try to intimidate him or from sheer stupidity by laying such an unguarded weapon so close to him. Either way, Eric recognized its shape. It was a popular Russian made semi-automatic, AK-47 machine gun, an old Soviet model but still deadly, and familiar to Eric. Collecting his thoughts, Eric felt his wrists and hands becoming more slippery due to the mixing of his blood and sweat against the iron handcuffs. He also noticed that the ancient screws holding the two sides of his handcuffs together had loosened due to his constant movement. However, he only had a moment to notice this before the second bodyguard began his sexual assault. This time Eric felt his ass split open from the assault. His pain was so intense as to be almost unbearable. He had to fight through the pain to prevent himself from fainting.

Meanwhile, underneath his groans and screams, he was concentrating on working his more and more slippery wrists and hands free. But no matter how he twisted his hands, the ancient cuffs were too tight for his hands to slip through. Finally, while the three rapists were totally focused on enjoying themselves by brutally violating him to prove their dominance and power over a hated Israeli, Eric thought of a desperate new strategy. He pretended to faint. He forced his body to go limp—preventing himself from groaning, screaming, or struggling. Al Kaduna's reaction was immediate. He announced in Arabic, "Well, this is no fun. I thought this guy would have more stamina. Unchain him, turn him over to face me, and bend his legs back over him. I want to see his face now that it's my turn. I know how to wake him up!" The two guards quickly followed their commander's orders. Eric could feel the ancient cuffs being removed from his wrists and ankles. He knew he only had seconds before the two guards would turn him over and hold him down for Al Kaduna. So, before any of his tormentors knew what was happening, he quickly reached out, grabbed the machine gun laying by his side and swung around, spraying multiple automatic rounds at point blank range—killing the two guards instantly—the bullets at that range almost severing their bodies in half. Their blood and guts splattered everywhere. Some deeply hidden part of Eric actually enjoyed this killing moment. As he pointed the machine gun at the shocked commander, Al Kaduna quickly fell to his knees, throwing his hands in the air in surrender, begging for his life.

Eric ordered him in Arabic, "Drop the pistol in your belt on the floor, or I'll blow your head off!" Al Kaduna immediately complied. Eric was free. Surprisingly, though, the main question in the back of his mind besides getting himself and the hostages out of there was how the hell was he going to explain his wounds to his married partner, Mark Cohn, who thought he was relaxing in a luxury Cairo hotel?

By questioning the commander, Eric confirmed Al Kaduna and his bodyguards were alone for the moment, guarding the prisoners, but more of his terrorist army would soon arrive and that the plane which brought them was parked on a nearby airfield. Al Kaduna also quickly revealed upon being questioned that he had the key to the next room where all Israeli male captives were being held.

Eric motioned with his machine gun for the commander to lead him to the room next door holding the imprisoned captives and unlock the door. The twelve Israeli men were already on their feet having heard Eric's screams and gun shots. As Al Kaduna unlocked their prison door, Eric yelled in Hebrew that it was time for them all to leave. When the door opened, the men took one look at Eric standing before them naked, bruised, and bleeding while holding a machine gun, and knew what had happened—no one said a word. They poured out of the room. Three of them were retired IDF officers, one a retired doctor/surgeon, and all had military training as is normal for Israelis. Eric told them there was another machine gun and a pistol on the floor in the next room, which they quickly retrieved. Eric, however, continued to question the commander in Arabic: first about where his military gear and clothes were and secondly where the women and children had been taken. As soon as he found his clothes, he pressed a hidden device alerting the Israeli military as to their exact location. He then found his comm link phone and alerted the military about their situation, saying all captives were alive and well. He also gave the Israeli military the location and the number of guards where the women and children were being held. Two minutes later, Israeli hunter-killer drones that had been in the area searching for the hostages were hovering overhead. They would be used to neutralize any terrorist reinforcements. Next, he announced to the group, "Within minutes there will be several Israeli attack and rescue helicopters carrying Israeli Special Forces arriving to rescue you." He then turned to the newly captive, kneeling, and bound commander of the terrorists. Eric, still feeling the intense burning rectal pain this man had inflicted on him seriously thought about executing him on the spot— in fact it took all his will power not to blow his head off. Certainly, none of the captives would have objected. Instead, he made a calculated decision that his prisoner would make a more valuable captive for more intel or even to trade.

While they waited for the helicopters to arrive, a recent captive, Daniel Mordecai, approached Eric and introduced himself as a retired doctor and surgeon. He gently told Eric, "Don't worry, but you are going to faint soon due to the loss of blood trickling down your legs. But I heard through the wall what happened to you and will be there to direct the medics as to the correct procedures. I promise to stay by your side to oversee all medical procedures." Eric could hear the Israeli helicopters fast approaching when he turned to face the doctor, just before he collapsed into his arms. On the lead helicopter were his comrades from Sayeret Matkal, itching for another fight with the terrorists and getting their comrade and hostages safely back. When they arrived, Eric's comrades where happy to see Eric alive but disappointed that the sight and sound of so many military Israeli helicopters and drones had caused the approaching terrorist reinforcements to halt and melt into the jungle. There would be no revenge firefight for them that day.

Eric awoke in the Sheba Medical Center hospital in Israel.

The room was antiseptically white and clean. His first thought was, *What a different atmosphere compared to an old slave prison in the middle of the jungle.* He noticed his wrists and hands were bandaged but then also noticed his partner, Mark Cohn, asleep, sitting up in a chair near him. He tried to move but found his whole body ached too much from his recent ordeal. So, he just stared at Mark, the love of his life, sleeping in a chair, wondering how he was going to explain all this to him. Just then the nurse entered, announcing she was glad to see that Eric was awake but accidentally waking Mark too.

The newspapers were full of the story. Eric was a national hero. All the captives had been freed with no one hurt. And it was all due to Eric's fast thinking and heroic actions. As soon as Mark awoke and saw Eric, he rushed to Eric's bedside, hugging him as gently as possible. Even so, Eric winced upon contact, so Mark quickly backed away. When their eyes met, they both started to cry in sweet relief. Mark always brought out the kinder, gentler side of Eric. Mark gently leaned his head on Eric's shoulder. The nurse, seeing this, left and stood guard outside the hospital room, giving them some much needed privacy. Before Eric could say anything, Mark softly told Eric, "Don't worry. I have been fully briefed on what happened to you. Let's concentrate on getting you better." But once the nurse had alerted the hospital doctor that Eric was awake, she could only give them a few precious minutes before she had to give way. Everyone wanted to speak to Eric. Besides Mark, the first in the room was the Director of the Mossad, Alon Reuben, followed by Major General Chiam Savage, in charge of Israel's Special Forces. Since Eric was technically on loan from the Israeli Special Forces to the Mossad, this hostage rescue was considered a combined operation. Next, Eric's friend and immediate boss in the Mossad, Colonel Sam Reichman entered the room. Lastly, Dr. Jacoby, Eric's assigned hospital doctor followed. The room was getting very crowded and noisy-everyone wanting to talk at the same time.

CHAPTER TWO

POST-TRAUMATIC STRESS DISORDER

Two days ago, before all this happened, Mark Cohn was having a perfectly normal day at their beautiful home near Caesarea, Israel. He was engrossed in research for their upcoming archeological expedition to find the ancient Jerusalem Temple treasure described in the famous Copper Scroll, a scroll made of copper found amongst the even more famous Dead Sea Scrolls written on parchment. Mark knew the discovery of the Temple treasure would cap an illustrious career of archeological discoveries. Mark's luck in finding things had led him to discover pinprick-sized holes shown on the photos of the back of the Copper Scroll, that when connected formed directional lines, which could be transferred to the front side, connecting different locations. As Mark studied detailed photographs of the Copper Scroll, since the actual one is kept in a museum in Jordan, he realized the person or persons who had created it were no ordinary ancient Judean citizens. The authors must have been Temple accountants with near-genius IQs who could keep track of the immense Temple wealth, and if asked today, could also easily solve a modern day Rubik's Cube puzzle within minutes. In fact, Mark recognized he was trying to solve an ancient treasure map written on copper and put together like a Rubik's Cube puzzle. This was the key to solving the puzzle of the scroll: what was north was really south; what was back was really front; and key directions should be read in reverse like looking through a mirror. It took all of Mark's concentration to unravel this—step by step.

Moreover, the authors of the scroll had used many words in ancient Hebrew that were not mainstream. Mark was sure that the use of ancient Hebrew slang words by such literate priests was meant to misdirect and confuse readers. There were several key words Mark was having trouble translating and was getting impatient for Eric with his fantastic linguistic abilities to return and help. Actually, he counted on Eric to double check all his research to make sure the expedition did not turn into a wild goose chase. However, he had not heard from Eric for several days, but he wasn't yet worried. Mark knew that sometimes Eric got so engrossed with his other "egghead" archeological expert friends that he would forget about everything else, including calling Mark to check in. Moreover, Mark understood Eric's absentmindedness, as he himself could get so wrapped up in his own projects that he sometimes lost track of time as well. Thus, Mark was half expecting Eric to open the front door either today or tomorrow with an apology and a big hug and kiss for not calling. Either that or an urgent call from Eric at the airport saying that he had forgotten to call ahead of time, but could Mark please drop everything and come pick him up?

So, Mark was a little surprised when Sam Reichman, their friend and expedition team member from previous treasure hunts, knocked on their door. The instant he looked at Sam's face he knew something was wrong but couldn't quite understand it. Sam was also Eric's former boss, a colonel in the Mossad. But Mark knew Eric and Sam had both retired from there so that couldn't be it. All Sam said was, "Eric is doing fine, but I have to drive you to the Sheba Medical Center right away." He wouldn't say anything more to Mark on the way to the hospital, suspecting Mark would be furious when he discovered Eric was working directly for the Mossad and Israeli Special Forces again when he got hurt rescuing the hostages. Mark's anxiety level further increased when they entered through a special entrance at the hospital guarded by a dozen soldiers.

Before Mark was allowed to see Eric, he was given a full briefing by Eric's chief doctor and surgeon, Dr. Daniel

Mordecai, on what had happened to Eric while in Africa. The vicious rape had been withheld from the newspapers and general public. But the military authorities, which included the Israeli Special Forces, the Mossad, and Defense Ministry had concurred with Eric's medical doctors that Eric was going to need long-term therapy for the trauma he had experienced, and that Mark would be critical in a successful recovery. So, it was felt that Mark should know everything from the start. This completely surprising information hit Mark like a brick to the side of the head.

Mark was devastated when he heard that not only had Eric lied to him about going on a mission like this in the first place, but that Eric and been captured, brutally raped, and almost died in a remote jungle. The fact that Eric's actions had saved all the hostages didn't enter into Mark's thinking. All Mark could think about was that the love of his life and trusted married partner had lied to him and then almost savagely died. These thoughts kept swirling around in his head. He was glad he was seated in Dr. Mordecai's office because he was feeling a little lightheaded when he heard the news. Dr. Mordecai continued to explain, "It is no coincidence that I am Eric's chief doctor on this case, even though I had recently retired as Director of Surgery at the Sheba Medical Center. My wife and I were part of the group of Israeli tourists kidnapped and then rescued by Eric. I strongly believe that my wife and I owe our lives to him. So I have returned to work to head the team of doctors that operated on Eric. I promised Eric in the jungle I would do this and I have kept my promise." He went on to explain, "Not only was the surgery completely successful but because Eric is in such excellent physical shape, I project Eric's physical recovery from his wounds to be relatively short—about two months or less. Eric has also been given all the appropriate blood tests to check for any venereal disease or AIDS. Everything came back negative. However, I am worried about Eric's emotional and mental state as a post-rape victim. I am worried that Eric could suffer from post-traumatic stress disorder or PTSD. So therefore, because of the circumstances, the military will order Eric to go through a series of psychoanalytic tests and follow up with support therapy and your involvement and support will be critical."

During Dr. Mordecai's explanation about Eric's situation, Mark felt sections of his brain return to focus. He realized he didn't care one bit about the lie Eric had told him. Mark knew that, in a sense, Eric was married to the Mossad before Eric met him—the kind of marriage no one ever really leaves. Besides, because of the difference in their ages, Mark was acutely aware that Eric already had his own life. He told himself to clear his mind, the love of his life needed him, and he would be there for him no matter what. The most important thing in his life now was that Eric was still alive. Mark responded, "I want to thank you, Dr. Mordecai, for all your help and support you gave Eric, but I can't wait to see him any longer. I have to see him now without delay." As he walked through the hospital corridors to Eric's room, Mark concluded that Eric may have his black side, but he was a rock that Eric could lean on now. With that thought, Mark entered Eric's hospital room. Outside the room in the corridor, there were another six IDF soldiers standing guard. Mark didn't know it then, but these were Eric's comrades from the Israeli Special Forces. When he saw Eric lying in his hospital bed, still asleep but bandaged and with IV tubes sticking in him, Mark surprised himself. Instead of fainting or crying or in any way melting, he resolved to make Eric well, no matter what! He also made a quiet promise to himself, "No more government missions of any kind for Eric." Mark meant to put his foot down hard this time. But for now, all he did was check with the nurses and floor doctor as to what was happening versus what was supposed to be happening concerning Eric's care. Eric's health advocate had arrived, and soon the entire nursing staff on the floor knew it.

CHAPTER THREE

THE POLITICIAN

As for the people crowding into Eric's hospital room as soon as Eric woke up, Mark really did not know or care who they were. No polite introductions were made. His main priority was getting Eric well and getting him home as soon as possible. Mark stood by Eric's bedside as his visitors showered Eric with congratulations on rescuing the hostages. Mark had positioned his body on purpose alongside Eric's bed but also between Eric and his visitors who were at the foot of the bed. His military visitors were getting a strong feeling that Mark's presence during this hospital room meeting was intrusive.

Eric, who by now was fully conscious and awake, was also able to read the slight tension in the room caused by Mark's protective presence. So, he gently but firmly said to Mark, "There is no reason to hide this from you anymore, but I need to be debriefed about this mission, and could you please leave the room while this is happening?" Mark was a little taken aback by this straightforward request, but he immediately acquiesced and departed. The next to leave Eric's room was Dr. Jacoby, who was also in charge of Eric's post-operative care. Mark was glad that he had a chance to speak to Dr. Jacoby alone in the hospital hallway. Dr. Jacoby appeared to Mark as a young, highly committed doctor, about Mark's height, with a full, dark brown beard.

Trying unsuccessfully to hide his anxiety, Mark asked, "I just want to know when Eric can come home?"

To which Dr. Jacoby replied, "Eric can go home when he is unhooked from the IV tube and can sit up, walk and urinate by himself. After checking on him tonight, assuming by then everything looks good, I will order the IV removed early tomorrow morning. He will then be released from the hospital tomorrow afternoon. However, Eric will have to be on strong stool softeners while his anal stitches heal. Eric's surgeon used disappearing stitches so there will be no need for a return trip to the hospital to remove them." He further added, "Eric's surgeon, Dr. Mordecai, is a genius. He put Eric back together as good as new. I will also give you a list of post-operative care instructions."

Mark responded, "I am so relieved that he can leave so soon. We both know that people only really start to get better when they go home from a hospital."

During their conversation, Mark noticed the intense interest of the military personnel who were guarding Eric.

Mark thought he could detect that they were straining to hear every word the doctor said to him. There were six of them. Finally, one of them introduced himself as Sergeant Isaac Caveda. He said that they were all members of Eric's squad in the Sayeret Matkal, or Israeli Special Forces, and very concerned about Eric. As they all introduced themselves, Mark realized he was getting a glimpse into Eric's hidden life. Mark also noticed that they were all wearing maroon colored berets, which were different from the light green IDF berets. To Mark, who had not yet finished processing that Eric still worked for the military, this accidental hallway meeting of his military comrades was a surprising and astounding development, especially since they all seemed to know about him and Eric. Mark thought that it was oddly funny that they all were as curious about him as he was about them. Since they all were intensely interested in Eric's health, Mark graciously said, "As soon as the big shots leave, you are all invited to visit Eric in his hospital room."

Almost in unison they all said, "Thank you, Sir."

Mark immediately understood that the use of the word, "Sir" was both very polite and a military term. Nevertheless it made him feel old compared to these young military "studs."

When the other visitors had left Eric's room after his debriefing, Mark, as promised, invited Eric's Special Forces comrades to visit with Eric. While in Eric's hospital room, Mark stood back and watched their interaction. It was very apparent to Mark that they all had a special camaraderie and were all a kind of family. Eric's military comrades were all young and in excellent physical shape. Sergeant Isaac Caveda was from Ethiopia—gregarious, tall, and a very handsome African man who seemed to Mark to have a close or even special relationship with Eric. He appeared to stand close, even too close to Eric in his bed, almost hovering over him. He was part of Beta Israel: Jews from Ethiopia who claim descent from Solomon and Sheba. Isaac was also fluent in Amharic, the official language of Ethiopia and very useful to know in Central Africa. Omri was a Mizrahi Jew, descended from Jewish North African immigrants and who enjoyed practicing his Arabic with Eric. The other four were Ashkenazi or European descended Israelis, with one almost as blond as Eric. Mark also learned that Eric's nickname in the group was "the Professor" because of his proficiency in several languages and the fact that he was also a few years older. If it had not been for the seriousness of Eric's recovery, Mark would have enjoyed this chance meeting much more. Also, he could not help but notice the distinct and somewhat intoxicating, sexual aroma of male testosterone that filled the room.

While standing by the side of Eric's hospital bed, Isaac did something very surprising in front of Mark and everyone.

He sang "Hatikvah," the stirring Israeli national anthem loud enough for the whole hospital floor to hear. It is a beautiful song based on nineteenth century romantic poetry describing the desire for the Jews to return to their homeland. He had an incredibly beautiful male singing voice, and all the nurses on the floor came and stared at him. In fact, the women were in awe of this very handsome black military man. All eyes were focused on him. Halfway through the song, he reached out and touched Eric's arm while Eric lay in his hospital bed. When he did this, Eric glanced at Mark for a split second. He saw that Mark was intently watching the "show." He also knew that Mark had seen what must have seemed to Mark like his "guilty glance."

As they were all saying good-bye when they left the hospital room after about twenty minutes of good-natured male banter, the kind that only men who have been under the most extreme physical and emotional tests together can relate, Isaac looked Mark straight in the eyes and said, "You are very lucky to have such a loving relationship with the Professor."

Mark noticed a very soft undertone of wistfulness or longing through the broad smile and pleasant good-bye. After they all departed and before Eric fell asleep, Eric commented from his hospital bed, "I am happy that you finally met my army buddies. It is not often we all can get together off base." He then quickly fell asleep as he was still not fully recovered from his ordeal.

As Mark looked upon the sleeping love of his life, a thought crept over him that he could not dismiss. *What is the real relationship between Eric and Isaac? Isaac is much closer to Eric's age and like Eric is in super physical shape. And there must be a great deal of downtime on these secret missions.* Trying hard not to feel jealous, Mark still knew that Isaac was unusually attached to Eric. As Mark fell asleep that night watching Eric in his bed, his thoughts were on this short encounter with Eric's military comrades. This interlude was a lot to take in for Mark and he wasn't sure he was thinking clearly considering the circumstances of Eric's near-death experience.

The next morning the nurse came into the room and unhooked Eric from everything. While they were waiting for Eric to be released from the hospital, Eric turned to Mark and asked him straight out if there was anything Mark wanted to discuss. Mark knew that Eric had purposefully kept his eyes from connecting with Isaac yesterday because Mark was watching, and that Mark had noticed this odd interaction. So, Mark took a chance, just to see Eric's reaction, and softly asked if Eric was aware that Isaac was in love with him. Mark added, "I am not surprised because falling in love with you is easy."

In response, Eric stood up, walked over to Mark, took Mark in his arms, and repeated their wedding vows: "You are mine and I am yours forever."

As usual, Mark felt himself melt in Eric's arms. Eric always knew exactly what to say to Mark. Still, there was a small part of Mark that remained unsatisfied with Eric's strong gesture of love, but not necessarily fidelity. However, Mark kept this thought to himself. Mark knew jealousy was so unbecoming in a relationship. Just as Eric buried his dark side for Mark's sake, so Mark decided to bury his extremely jealous side too.

Sam drove them both home that afternoon. Mark was surprised to see two IDF soldiers stationed at the bottom hill where their driveway began. Sam, who was in a great mood because his friend Eric was returning home, simply said just before they arrived, "Don't worry about the guards posted at the bottom of the hill. They will be there for a while for your safety." Both guards waved and smiled as they passed. Sam also said Jacob, who lived at the top of the hill on the same road, had also approved the guards to be temporarily stationed there. However, both Sam and Eric noticed something was different with Mark now that the medical crisis had passed. And in spite of Mark's best efforts to hide it and deal with it, he was still furious at Eric for lying to him. And both Eric and Sam read him!

Sam helped get Eric into the house and into bed. Mark was really looking forward to being alone with Eric. Another surprise for both Eric and Mark but an understandable one was that Eric would have to sleep in his own room in his own bed until Eric recovered. Just before Sam was about to leave, a registered nurse named Zelda arrived to make sure everything was set up properly and informed Eric and Mark she would be there for an eight hour shift every day until the doctor ordered her to stop. Two minutes later, Eric's mother, Miriam, and brother, David Jansen, arrived followed by Jacob Kurtz, their billionaire friend and neighbor, and his chef, Noah. Noah, who was also Mark and Eric's part-time chef, carried platters of already prepared food. He headed directly to the kitchen while Eric's mother made a beeline for Eric.

She embraced her son lying on his bed and said, "I am so proud of you. The papers are full of you rescuing the hostages. But the doctors wouldn't let me visit in the hospital." She was distressed to see his hands bandaged, but Zelda interjected.

"Don't worry, his surgeon used a new technique so that his hands will heal quicker, and after a few months, there won't even be any scars." His mother was so relieved and happy to hear this. Also, like most of Israel, she had no idea about the rape.

Mark pointedly asked Eric's brother David, also a military man, if he knew Eric was going on this dangerous mission. All he said was, "I couldn't stop him." By saying this in front of his mother, Miriam, and Mark, he had, in effect, "thrown Eric under the bus" when they both turned and looked straight at Eric—both surprised that Eric's brother knew he had volunteered for this dangerous mission, and they didn't. Eric had also told his mother the lie that he had retired from such assignments. So, Eric knew that his manipulations had caught up with him and was more than a bit embarrassed. On that note, Sam said good-bye to everyone and departed, leaving Eric to face the music alone and not wanting to get in the middle of a possible family quarrel.

About twenty minutes later, Mark could see Eric was getting tired. So, Mark stood up and thanked everyone for coming, but it was time for them to leave, Eric needed rest. By the time everyone, including the nurse, had departed, Eric had fallen asleep. As Mark returned to Eric's room, he decided to sleep in the big easy chair next to him that night, just in case Eric needed something during the night.

Mark awoke the next morning to Eric emerging from the bathroom. Mark immediately noticed that normal color had returned to Eric's face. Mark and Eric stood in the bedroom and just hugged one another—needing to feed off each other's energy. Both so different but so perfectly matched, a true yin and yang relationship.

Finally, Mark said, "The doctors say that physically you will heal as good as new, but they are worried about your emotional and mental state after the rape."

Eric looked Mark straight in the eyes when he replied in a tone Mark had never heard Eric use before. "I made sure the people who raped me will never rape anyone again. And really, I'm fine." Eric meant to let Mark see his steely black side but only for a moment. Eric could tell Mark understood and was a little taken aback. So, to lighten the mood, Eric then said while pressing against Mark, "Since I have two bandaged hands, I am going to need someone to handle things down there for me."

Mark immediately replied with a smile, "As you know, I am really good at handling that thing down there." They both started to laugh. Mark instinctively knew that laughter was the best therapy for Eric and was glad Eric was again feeling frisky and that his goofy sense of humor had returned.

It was now Mark's turn to be serious. He told Eric, "For the record, I have completely forgiven you this time for lying to me about going on this secret military mission. I realize you lied to me so I wouldn't worry."

Eric immediately understood when Mark emphasized the words "this time." He knew it meant there had better not be any more times or lies.

Nurse Zelda arrived about five minutes later, saying, "I almost didn't get through the crowd and guards at the bottom of the hill, but they finally found my name on the list."

Mark stopped and turned, asking, "There's a list to get in here and a crowd outside?" He was surprised to hear this.

About 10:00 a.m., Jacob Kurtz came to visit again with his chef Noah close behind. Even before saying hello, he stated, "You both better get used to Noah bringing food everyday while Eric is convalescing. No thanks necessary. It is my pleasure to help. But I want to talk about something important."

When they were seated in the living room, he asked, "Are you both aware that there is a huge crowd at the bottom of the hill just waiting to see Eric?" They both said they had just heard about it but had not been outside the house today. Jacob leaned slightly forward in his seat before he next spoke. Mark always knew when Jacob sat forward something important was coming. Jacob now paused as if collecting his thoughts. Then asked, "Eric, have you ever thought of going political—running for public office?" Both Eric and Mark gave each other a surprised look for a brief second.

Then Eric replied with Mark nodding in agreement, "Yes, I am interested and curious. Perhaps I would be able to help my country?" What he didn't say publicly was that part of him—Mark called it his black side— had always been fascinated by the concept of power and its use.

So, Jacob continued, "I have recently had conversations with some very deep pocketed money men, me included, who would back you financially if you ever decided to run for office. They rightfully think you are a national military hero. And if you both don't believe me, then Eric just show yourself to the crowd at the foot of the hill and see their reaction."

Mark asked Eric if he felt well enough for a short walk outside to test what Jacob just said. Nurse Zelda immediately intervened, saying Eric was still not well enough for that but could go in a wheelchair for a short time.

Eric rejected the wheelchair idea, saying, "I don't want the public to see me in a wheelchair." This time, both Jacob and Mark looked at one another, recognizing Eric's natural political instinct. Eric then asked, "If you both don't mind, nurse Zelda can push me in the wheelchair to the front door, then when I get up, you both can stand at each side for support in case I need it." Mark and Zelda immediately agreed and were curious to see what would happen.

When Eric reached the front door in his wheelchair, he stood up, walked out the front door, faced the crowd, and instinctively raised his bandaged hands above his head, more in a gesture of triumph than to wave. Mark, in disbelief, stepped back and looked up at both Eric's hands above his head making the *V* for victory sign with his two figures clearly visible above his bandages. The crowd went wild, clapping and chanting Eric's name in unison. There must have been over hundred people in the crowd. Eric breathed in the power of the crowd's adulation. It was apparent he loved it as he flashed his movie star smile. This only lasted for a few minutes before Eric signaled he needed to go inside again. Meanwhile, Mark realized while standing by Eric that the two soldiers last night had grown to six but still might not be enough to control this very large crowd of Eric's enthusiastic admirers, including the press.

When inside the house again, nurse Zelda insisted that Eric rest in bed. While the nurse was tending to Eric in his room, Jacob, who had watched this show from the shadows inside the house and who was now alone with Mark, turned to him and said, "Did you hear it?"

Mark replied, "Hear what?"

Then, Jacob looked straight at Mark and said, "The door that just opened and the door that just closed! Meaning a new political career has just been born and Eric's old life will inevitably change."

Mark immediately understood and agreed that Jacob's insight was correct but inwardly had his doubts about how this change would affect his future relationship with Eric.

Jacob looked at Mark and said, " I am going to make this happen!"

CHAPTER FOUR

THE ROAD TO JERUSALEM

Israel now had its military hero and sex symbol rolled into one. During the next few weeks, events happened fast. Wherever they went, the crowds got bigger and bigger. The press wouldn't leave them alone. Mark needed to process it. Eric seemed to flourish in the spotlight, not officially running for public office but nevertheless creating a draft situation where he would reluctantly accept a nomination if called. Jacob created this strategy with Eric's enthusiastic approval and support. There was a constant parade to their home of military officers, politicians, union heads, not to mention the leader of every political party in the Knesset and US and Russian embassy representatives to ostensively give Eric their good wishes on his safe return and thank him for his daring hostage rescue but really to get a "read" on this rising star. Eric had almost completely physically healed and would very soon be on a normal schedule. He had started a full workout schedule in their private gym and was also swimming laps again in their pool. Lovemaking between Mark and Eric was frequent but a different story. Eric had become much more aggressive and not as gentle as before. Nevertheless, they were sleeping in the same bed again. And that was the reason Mark insisted that they both attend all the military mandated counseling sessions for PTSD victims. Actually, they both noticed the change in their lovemaking, and both wanted to understand it so that they could fix it.

That's when they met Lieutenant Colonel Rachel Stein, senior psychologist for the IDF and specializing in Mossad operatives. She first seemed to Mark as sort of a mother earth figure—somewhat overweight, short, with a really big bosom and about fifty years old with an extremely ingratiating personality. But Mark and Eric both soon realized she was an iron fist in a velvet glove and eerily insightful. Her one goal was to make Eric well again.

After several counseling sessions, they discovered that Eric was still furious with himself about being violated during the rape and not blowing the commander's head off when he had the chance. Even though Eric was very aware that by not killing the commander, it had led to some very vital intel about the terrorist group and the location of the female hostages. Thus, Eric's conscious mind knew it was the correct decision. Additionally, Eric still felt personally angry and guilty for stupidly allowing himself to be captured and raped in the first place. They also discovered that Eric had an extreme "risk taking personality." However, that bit of news did not come as a surprise to them. Now that Eric and Mark knew what was causing the problem, both set out to solve it. According to Lieutenant Colonel Stein, it would take many more professional counseling sessions in addition to their steadfast mutual love. Thus, they were all committed to getting Eric completely cured no matter how long it took.

Moreover, Mark was also gaining some insight into the split personality of the warrior spy he had married. During the therapy session, Eric soon realized why he loved Mark so much. It happened when Mark firmly stated, "It was a good thing the terrorist commander who orchestrated Eric's rape had just been sentenced to death by an Egyptian court. Otherwise, I would kill him myself!" When Eric heard this, he realized immediately that Mark was no killer. Eric sat silently, just smiling. Because Eric, himself, had realized long ago that he was! Eric also became aware during therapy that he had to become satisfied with the death sentence and the brutal Egyptian prison conditions for Al Kaduna while he awaited execution. He had to get control of his urge to murder Al Kaduna in revenge. Lieutenant Colonel Stein also strongly recommended they both take a vacation away from Israel to change scenes and do some much needed healing. In fact, her request sounded like an order. Throughout these sessions, though, Eric was always careful to keep control of his public emotional revelations about himself— fearing that if he ever revealed the full extent of his hunter, killer black side, it would rupture his relationship with Mark. However, Eric did not worry about revealing too much of himself to Lieutenant Colonel Stein because his instinct told him she already knew exactly who he was and of what he was capable. Back home, Mark also noticed there was a change in Eric's interests. Eric no longer was passionate about archeology. During his period of convalescence, Eric helped Mark translate the words on the Copper Scroll that needed translating and clearly decided where and how the treasure was hidden. Together they had a "Eureka moment" when they discovered the key to reading the scroll and realized the enormous Jerusalem Temple treasure had been hidden in plain sight all along. They both planned to give a dinner party to announce the discovery of the location of the treasure and how to read the scroll to their archeological team from previous expeditions within a week. They would organize a new treasure hunting expedition the next day after the announcement. But Mark sensed that Eric was bored with the translations and not excited about a possible major new archeological discovery. Eric's real passion now had become politics. Eric would rather give a speech at a political rally than a lecture about archeology. And they both still could not believe how popular Eric had become! Another major change in their lives was Eric had at last agreed that his days of an active soldier had ended. Mark had put his foot down on this point and Eric had finally officially retired from the military. This left Eric free to pursue politics. So much so that Mark wondered again who had managed who in their relationship. But it did not matter to Mark, because after all that had happened, they were still together and very much in love with each other.

Eric was now spending a great deal of time visiting the leaders of all the current political parties in Israel, many times bringing Mark with him to show their commitment to their gay marriage. It took Eric several months, but he became quite familiar with all the Israeli political parties, and more importantly, the personalities and interests of the men who controlled them. However, alongside all these new activities, Eric always found time to do his extreme daily gym workouts, keeping himself in battle ready shape. Mark approved of this since these workouts and military training exercises (due to his reserve status), seemed to relieve Eric's sometimes considerable tension.

One night he and Eric were invited to dinner at Jacob's Roman style villa at the top of the hill on the road where they lived. Mark thought the only odd thing about the invitation was that this time Jacob asked him to wear something extra nice because there would be other guests attending. Jacob's villa was so close to their house that Mark decided to walk it alone since Eric was already there. The other dinner guests were three of the richest men in Israel. No spouses except Mark had been invited. Mark had never met these men before. They were very charming and gracious to him when he was introduced. In fact, they went out of their way to compliment him on his fame as an archeologist and treasure hunter. Mark's instinct kicked in almost immediately. It told him that this dinner was really a very important, strategic political meeting for Eric and himself. He also knew when he was being "stroked" with all these compliments.

He didn't have long to wait to discover the real meaning of the dinner. There are six families in Israel who own everything worth owning. Their interests and holdings are global, and they are all immensely wealthy. The heads of three of those families plus Jacob, Mark, and Eric attended this dinner party. Mark had been to Jacob's house for dinner dozens of times. Moreover, all the dinners had been relaxed and informal— most often eating in their bathing suits from a buffet table— not this time. The dining room table had been set with a white tablecloth and the finest and most expensive porcelains and crystal goblets with beautiful orchids as a centerpiece. As Mark took his seat, he curiously tapped the gold colored place plate set before him. He realized it was made of solid gold! Spontaneously, Mark blurted out, "Now I know what happened to all the gold treasure Eric and I discovered!" The whole table burst into laughter. It broke the ice for the evening. Everyone became more relaxed. Soon after that, Jacob stood up to make a toast.

He held up his gold rimmed crystal goblet full of expensive wine and said, "Here's to the start of our new political party with Eric Jansen as its leader!"

Mark's jaw dropped as everyone clapped and he watched Eric stand to speak. While Eric spoke, Mark realized Eric had become a really great public speaker. He was the perfect candidate—a military hero with movie star looks and who also was a happily married gay man. They all knew that the gay marriage aspect of Eric's life was an issue on the religious right of Israeli politics but thought Eric was the one candidate who could surmount it. Before the end of dinner, all three men and Jacob decided to back Eric for public office—perhaps one day for prime minister!

In the meantime, Eric's therapy sessions had proceeded as planned with Eric mentally healing from his ordeal. Or, at least, this was what Mark hoped. As Eric planned his next political move, Mark was putting together an archeological expedition to follow the map where the Temple treasure mentioned in the Copper Scroll was hidden. Everything was going great for the two men until one night. Eric had tossed and turned so much that he woke Mark. In fact, Eric thrashed his arms so violently that he almost hit Mark in the face. Missed him by an inch. When Mark woke Eric from his nightmare, Eric was extremely apologetic and slept normally through the remainder of the evening. In the morning, Mark thought the episode was a PTSD relapse. But it wasn't. The next night was almost the same with Eric tossing and turning all night.

Two nights later in their home, Mark and Eric were supposed to host a dinner party to celebrate the kickoff of the new treasure hunting expedition they were planning. The first logistical meeting of the new archeological expedition was scheduled for the next morning. Key team members from previous successful treasure hunting expeditions were due to attend both. This included Sam Reichman, Ariel Kurtz and his wife Julie, Jethro, Noah, Solomon Levine and Jacob Kurtz.

Mark had cooked a special meal for the event. It took two days of preparation. Not only was there going to be the excitement and fun of an important announcement at dinner about their next treasure hunt, but Mark seriously thought that tasty, home cooked food, with some of Eric's favorite dishes, surrounded by old friends would help ease Eric's PTSD. He prepared Eric's favorite paprika chicken with a side dish of roasted butternut squash with a shot of Madeira (Portuguese wine—Mark's secret ingredient), poured over it at the last minute as well as a side dish of whipped sweet potatoes. First, there would be plenty of homemade hummus and falafel as well as three different Israeli salads from which to choose, plus plenty of champagne, wine and vodka. For dessert, Noah baked homemade chocolate rugalach— a bite-size Danish, also a spiced honey date cake with caramel sauce, and finally, a fresh angel food cake, over which Mark insisted on pouring a shot of Grand Marnier liqueur with optional whipped cream. Mark enjoyed cooking with plenty of alcohol. His entertainment philosophy was that even if his dinner guests didn't like the food, at least they would leave "happy."

However, Eric was late to arrive for dinner. Mark thought he had gotten caught up in some political event or meeting. When Eric walked in the door and greeted everyone, they all stared. Eric had dyed his yellow blond hair on his head, eyebrows and recent very short beard, dark brown. Everyone was stunned by his new look but complimented Eric that he was still movie star handsome with dark hair. Everyone complimented him but Sam Reichman, who was also a retired Mossad officer. He could read the "signs." All he said to Eric was, "When are we leaving?"

Eric replied, "I am leaving by myself very early tomorrow morning."

Upon hearing the serious tone of this conversation, everyone fell dead silent. The mood of the evening completely changed. Mark got his bearings just enough to say, "I apologize to everyone, but I need to ask you to please leave. You all will be invited back for dinner another night. Additionally, I will make the announcement about the new expedition site another time. And I am also postponing the archeological logistical meeting scheduled for tomorrow."

Everyone quickly departed except Sam. When the front door closed behind the last guest, Sam turned to Eric and said, "You didn't tell Mark, did you?"

Eric hesitated so Sam informed Mark, "The terrorist responsible for the kidnapping of the hostages and Eric's rape and torture, Mohammed Al Kaduna, escaped from an Egyptian jail four days ago. He was sentenced to death by an Egyptian court and killed two Egyptian guards during his escape. The entire Egyptian army and police are looking for him."

To this Eric replied, "They are looking in the wrong places."

Sam quickly added, "Eric's dark hair will make him less conspicuous if we have to hunt Africa's most wanted terrorist undercover across Africa."

Mark instantly connected this news to Eric's nightmares. So, he thought he remained remarkably calm when he asked

Eric, "Do you remember that you promised me and your mother that you had retired from the Mossad and would no longer go on any government sponsored dangerous missions?" Mark realized, however, based on Eric's body language, the look on Eric's face and tone of voice that this was going to happen regardless of any previous promises. He also realized it might bring Eric closure if he could hunt and kill this terrorist who had tortured him. So, Mark quickly added, "However, because this is a special case, I know you have to do this on a personal level, and I support your decision no matter what." However, Mark felt the feeling of dread building inside him for his partner's safety.

Eric then turned to Sam and said, "Sam, if you want to tag along so badly, you can meet me at the Tel Aviv airport tomorrow at 5:00 a.m. for a flight to Cairo connecting through Athens. But I am only going to use the old ways this time."

As Eric said this, Mark could feel the animal energy of the two men rising in front of him as if he was looking at two lions pacing back and forth preparing for a blood hunt.

Just before Sam was about to leave to prepare for their journey, Mark asked Eric what he meant by using the "old ways." Eric hesitated.

So Sam answered with a slight smile on his lips and with a tone he had never heard Sam use before. "The old ways mean that Eric is going to use knives to get up close and personal, no guns unless he has no choice." It was an utterly ferocious side of Sam and Eric that Mark had never seen. Then Sam said, "I have to hurry if I am going to meet Eric at the Tel Aviv airport." He then turned and abruptly closed the door behind him. Afterwards, Mark felt that he was beginning to get much deeper insights into the warrior spy he'd married.

As soon as Sam departed and Mark and Eric were alone, but before Mark could say a word, Eric grabbed Mark and started to make love to him. It was not a gentle lovemaking but a fierce, animal lovemaking. Mark knew that when Eric got tense and excited, like after sky diving, Eric needed to release his tensions by making love like this, and they both immensely enjoyed it. Eric also knew that making love like this would put Mark into a deep relaxed sleep. Eric counted on it. Afterwards as expected, he quickly left the house while Mark was in a deep sleep to begin his hunt for the escaped terrorist.

Mark slept until late morning before waking up to an empty house with the lights on from the night before and untouched food on the table ready to be eaten like a still life painting of an abandoned dinner party.

Mark walked around in a bit of a daze, taking stock of all that had happened last night. After about a half hour, he found himself standing in the middle of his living room in an empty house just staring out to the pool. As his thoughts clarified, he knew he needed to call all his friends and apologize for ending the dinner party so abruptly. But his instinct told him to call Jacob Kurtz first. Jacob, his wealthy neighbor and friend who Mark knew had contacts into everything important in the country. He thought Jacob could discover or possibly already knew what Eric was doing and if he needed back up. In fact, Mark thought he was going to walk to his neighbor's house and knock on the door. Formalities be damned! On the way, he thought about how everyone told him that Eric was so easy to get along with and relaxed about everything. Actually, Mark thought that Eric could be so damn difficult sometimes and he was worried sick about him!

Eric, meanwhile, had no intention of taking a flight to Cairo. It was a diversionary story for Mark and anyone else to which Mark happened to talk. He drove to a secret airbase in southern Israel used by Israeli Special Forces to board a military helicopter that would take him down the coast of the Gulf of Eilat, over the Red Sea and Southern Sudan to Juba, the capital of the Central African Republic. This long-range military helicopter was state of the art and a one of a kind prototype. Some said it was more like a spaceship that could take off and land vertically as well as hover or even float! The military weaponry on board was all laser, more accurate and deadly than machine guns or rocket launchers but completely silent. It was supposed to be the apogee of precision. It could maneuver like a dragonfly in flight at lightning speed. The engine, too, was powered by the same source that powered the lasers. It, theoretically, gave the helicopter unlimited travel range. Eric had spent the last two days reviewing the new helicopter's potential but yet untested capabilities in the field. Eric's research revealed how Israeli scientists had refined laser technology by fusing the strongest blue light wave into heat and then energy. This fusion power created clean hydrogen energy that could power an engine for flight as well as weapons that were so accurate they could light the tip of your cigar from a moving helicopter or destroy a city in just seconds. In fact, the soldiers of the Israeli Special Forces had named this new breed of helicopter *Dragonfly* to symbolize future change and acknowledge their new battleship helicopter was like a dragonfly which is one of the most accurate and deadly hunters in the insect world. Moreover, the element that brought *Dragonfly* squarely into the future of warfare occurred when its fusion engine was reversed and then reversed again at great speed, creating an anti-gravity field around the helicopter. Hence, rotor blades became superfluous—folding back and hidden inside its top when hovering or even flying! Thus, the rotor blades become a back-up system if needed. However, none of this or anything else on it had been tested yet in the real world and certainly not in actual combat. Just controlled tests under laboratory conditions. This covert mission was only supposed to test its long range flight and speed capabilities, nothing more.

They planned to land the helicopter close to the head waters of the White Nile where Eric guessed, but now confirmed by Israeli satellite imagery, that Al Kaduna would be hiding with possibly dozens of other terrorists. The final stage would still entail a grueling hike through thick jungle to get to the terrorists. Complicating the situation was that all the countries in this part of the world were in a state of perpetual civil war financed by what is called "blood diamonds or conflict diamonds," which are illegally mined diamonds used to fund terrorism around the world. And the Central African Republic was the center of such trade in diamonds regardless of any international agreements the government signed to prohibit it. So, Eric was glad to see Sam's friendly face already waiting for him on board the helicopter when he arrived.

All Sam said, "What kept you, Major Jansen?"

Eric replied, "Had to give Mark a proper good-bye, Colonel Reichman." At Eric's response, a knowing half smile appeared on both their faces.

CHAPTER FIVE

BIG GAME HUNTING

Sam yelled out to alert the commandos, "The Professor has arrived!" With that announcement, the most advanced prototype battleship helicopter in the world took off in seconds, moving with the speed and maneuverability of a dragonfly insect hovering above a lake on a hot summer's day looking for its prey. It was its first long range test run. The plan was to be just a quick covert tactical exercise to do a limited test of its flying capabilities. Most of its military weapons systems had not yet been fully tested. No one planned or wanted it to do anything more. Adding to the danger of this covert mission was a small chance that its new fusion anti-gravity engine could blow up with the power of a small hydrogen bomb if not operated properly. On board were Eric's six Special Forces teammates plus Sam, Eric, and two pilots, all officially volunteers. They all knew about Eric's capture and torture and the Israeli tourists' kidnapping and were all itching for payback.

Earlier the Israeli government had begrudgingly given their prisoner, Mohammed Al Kaduna to the Egyptian government for trial. The Egyptians had claimed the right to put him on trial in their country since the kidnapping of the bus of Israeli tourists had occurred on their soil. To keep peaceful relations between the two countries, Israel had agreed. Besides the Israeli government knew that Egypt has a death penalty for terrorism and kidnapping while officially Israel still does not. Capital punishment in Israel has only been imposed twice in the history of the state and was only handed out for treason and crimes against humanity.

When Mohammed Al Kaduna escaped, the Israeli government felt its deal with Egypt also ended. He became the most wanted terrorist in Africa and this time there would be no more deals for his life. Israel doesn't forget. In fact, the top command in Israel knew they could not stop Major Jansen from hunting Al Kaduna by himself. So, they decided to support him. This was a most official unofficial mission since Israel would have to violate several countries' sovereignty to successfully accomplish it. However, these official unofficial covert missions are par for the course for the Mossad and Sayeret Matkal. It also meant that the hunt was supported by Israeli satellite tracking imagery that is among the most exact on the planet. This was most important since it confirmed Eric's guess that Al Kaduna was again in the Central African Republic when it showed him getting out of a Jeep and entering a small house, more like a hut, in the middle of the jungle. It was Israel's assumption that most of the terrorist base was hidden, below ground, but only an assumption at this point.

Back home in Israel, Mark was so anxious about Eric's abrupt decision and departure to go on a revenge mission that he almost ran up the hill to Jacob's house. As he arrived, he noticed several cars parked in front of the house. He thought that Jacob must be having a meeting and if this had been a normal visit, Mark would never have bothered Jacob when he was busy. But this wasn't normal; it involved the life and death of his partner. So, Mark knocked hard on the big bronze double front doors of the house as well as pressing the buzzer several times with no response. Mark knew this house well. He had visited dozens of times. The house was huge and almost a perfect replica of a Roman villa fit for an ancient Roman senator or even a Caesar. The front of the house, except for the ten foot high double doors, was windowless. The blank facade gave no indication of the architectural masterpiece that lay beyond, with its beautiful, peristyle open air center court and fountain surrounded by dozens of Doric columns leading to coffered ceiling rooms full of art and beyond to a marble terrace with an infinity swimming pool looking over the shoreline vista of Israel. Mark also knew that if Jacob were in the rear of the house by the pool, he would never hear him knocking. Since Mark thought every moment counted in helping Eric, he went around to the side of the house where he knew there was a narrow trail with a moderately high but climbable fence blocking the way to the rear.

Under normal circumstances, Mark would never have allowed himself to do something so undignified as climbing a neighbor's security fence, but he was over the high fence and on the rear terrace in just a few minutes. He actually surprised himself with how easy the fence was to climb. He proceeded to walk around the house, noticing the empty pool terrace while looking into its rear windows. He then knocked on the French windows to get Jacob's attention. When he knocked the second time, he noticed four men, including Jacob, standing around a table reviewing some papers, motioning him to come in. Mark entered. As he approached Jacob, he immediately apologized, saying, "I am sorry for entering your house this way unannounced and also asking you to leave so abruptly last night at our dinner party."

Jacob responded to Mark, "There is certainly no problem as we were taking bets on whether or not you would be able to climb my security fence. We were all ready to run out and help if you got stuck on it. Gideon didn't think you could do it. He lost!"

At that point Mark thought he heard the man named Gideon, whom he had not formally met yet, mutter under his breath something like "Fucking fag." Under normal circumstances, Mark would have aggressively confronted the man about this. But Mark had more important things on his mind, so he paid no attention to it.

Jacob must have heard Gideon's comment but also chose to ignore it as he continued, "Mark, you must have forgotten that I have state of the art security cameras around the house, and you have been watched since you walked up the road!" Jacob then proceeded to introduce Mark to his three guests. First there was Gideon Avraham, the assistant director of the Mossad, then Major General Chiam Savage, head of the Sayeret Matkal (the Israeli Special Forces) and Shimon Weisman, the defense minister of Israel. The major general mentioned to Mark that they had seen each other in Eric's hospital room but had not been introduced. They were all being very polite, but Mark still felt embarrassed about his entrance.

As soon as the introductions were finished, Mark explained, "The reason for my brash entrance is my grave concern for my partner Eric Jansen. I don't know exactly where Eric is, but I am sure Eric has gone after Al Kaduna alone or maybe with Sam Reichman in Egypt or Africa somewhere. And I need to ask if any of you know about Eric and could you possibly help me and bring him back. If not, then I will volunteer to immediately fly to Cairo to help him because he is going to need back up." Mark also stated that he was not the normal stay at home spouse with which they were used to dealing.

In response, Gideon Avraham, the assistant director of the Mossad, said, "We were just talking about Eric's situation before you arrived."

With a nod from Jacob, Noah appeared with some iced tea, saying to Mark, "You look frazzled and possibly dehydrated from the run up the hill and climb over the fence, so please drink it." Mark thanked Noah for being so thoughtful and took a big gulp.

He then started to ask another question but before he could finish the sentence, he was out cold. Noah had drugged his drink. He woke up in a big bed in what looked to him like a very luxurious hotel room. Also, to his surprise, Alisa, Sam's wife was sitting in a chair reading the news on her iPhone at the other end of the room.

When she saw that he was awake, she said, "Hi, glad you're awake."

Mark, still a bit dazed, asked her, "What happened? Where am I? How long have I been asleep?"

Alisa replied, "They took you at your word that you were going to interfere in a highly sensitive operation, and they couldn't let that happen. So here you are for the remainder of the mission. Want something to eat? Oh, and you've been asleep for almost six hours and you're in one of Jacob's guest rooms."

The very next moment, Jacob entered the room. He started the conversation by complimenting Mark on being agile enough at Mark's age to scale his side gate and by doing so revealed a home security weakness, which he was having corrected as they spoke. He further continued, "The reason both of you are here is that I know you both are very worried about your spouses. I assure you that Eric and Sam are being monitored by satellite and are safe. And that this mission is completely voluntary, and they both are indeed retired from the Mossad but technically still in the reserves. So, it is simply what Israel calls an officially, unofficial covert mission. And we couldn't have Mark asking the wrong people questions about it in Cairo."

Both Mark and Alisa were silent, processing what Jacob had just told them. So, Mark asked Jacob, "What is your part in all this?"

Jacob replied, "I know everyone involved and I am trying to make sure everyone returns safe from a successful mission."

This answer seemed to satisfy Mark while Alisa just sat there and listened. Jacob was not going to confide in Mark about something of which Alisa was already well aware. That he was the director of a secret, supra-agency that coordinated and gave strategic direction to all Israel's intelligence and military agencies and that his film production company was a cover! Jacob also told them with a chuckle, "Don't worry about eating or drinking anything that Noah serves you. So, is everyone ready for some dinner?"

The untested and unusual helicopter silently landed without incident in the early morning in a small clearing outside Juba, the capital of the Central African Republic. The clearing was close to the head waters of the White Nile and the place where Israel had seen via satellite, Al Kaduna enter a hut, possibly leading to a hidden, below ground installation. All the crew and passengers had to strap themselves into specially designed seats in anticipation of withstanding the intense pressure of supersonic Mach 2 speed. However, they all were pleasantly surprised to learn that the new anti-gravity properties of the hydrogen fusion engine almost completely eliminated the intense interior cabin pressure while flying at supersonic speeds. So, they discovered that there was really no need for these specialized seats. Moreover, they had silently flown the distance of 1,908 miles between the two countries in a little more than one hour at Mach 2 supersonic speed—three times as fast as the fastest jet plane and six times the speed of the fastest helicopter. Additionally, its new hydrogen fusion engine had no pollution exhaust or sonic booms when it broke the sound barrier!

One of the commandos yelled to everyone on board, "I'm here so quick that I would not even have had enough time to finish reading today's *Jerusalem Post*." Everyone chuckled at this.

In response, Captain Gil Sofer, the senior pilot commented, "I think this is just cruising speed for *Dragonfly*. In fact, I think *Dragonfly* could easily reach Mach 6, which would make it possible for it to leave Earth's atmosphere and travel in space!" This stunned everyone.

Then, back to the business at hand, Sam and Eric called a brief strategy meeting. Sam let Eric lead the meeting, knowing Eric's outstanding hunting skills. Eric told the team of commandos and pilots, "I hope I am wrong, but I believe we are walking into a trap. It was just too easy to find and see Al Kaduna via satellite. He wants us to come. So, the best way to hunt him is to spring the trap. Sam has agreed to stay on board to take command if we come under fire. Previously, if what Captain Sofer told me about *Dragonfly* is only half accurate, it will be our secret weapon for our hunt. From here, it is about a five mile hike through thick jungle to the hut that Mohammed Al Kaduna entered. I'm sorry about that, but I did not want to land any closer for fear of discovery." He added one last order for the team before they started to jump, "No prisoners should be taken on this mission!"

Eric was the first of six Israeli commandos to jump off the helicopter and land on the ground, a distance of about five feet, to begin their assault. After they all landed safely, Eric yelled to the pilots, "Take off now!" The commandos then turned and quickly disappeared into the deep jungle in the direction of the terrorist base. The plan was for the helicopter to silently hover or more accurately float unseen in place just above the clouds so as not to alert any terrorists. The pickup spot would be at the same clearing six hours later. This allowed two hours to get to the destination, two hours there, and two hours to get back, a quick in and out surprise assault, unless changed by one side or the other due to extreme circumstances. The mission, once there, was not to engage except for the specific target, Al Kaduna, and once the target was terminated to unobtrusively leave. *Dragonfly* proceeded to perform another test by engaging its new fusion anti-gravity device, which silently and quickly lifted it above the billowy jungle clouds where it remained silently waiting, hidden from all.

The hike to their destination took just under two hours as estimated and was uneventful except, of course, for the living green hell they had to hike through to get there, or as the ecologists would say, through "an area of great biodiversity." Poisonous snakes, spiders, and insects were everywhere. There were blood sucking leeches in the foot deep muddy water areas, not to mention a wild pack of lions that had noticed their intrusion and seemed to be hunting them or at least taken a keen interest. Luckily, they found a path carved by small forest elephants who inhabit the densest jungles. Small because their miniature size gives them greater flexibility in the dense jungle underbrush. All this in almost 100 degree heat and humidity. But to top it all, was the fact that although heavily armed, they could not fire a single shot to protect themselves for fear of alerting the terrorists. When they reached the hut where satellites saw Al Kaduna enter, there were no fences or guards, just a dirt road wide enough for two cars leading into a large clearing. The jungle created its own security wall around the place. Fortunately, all the Israeli commandos had been inoculated against tropical illnesses.

There were a half dozen cars and trucks parked under the shade of the jungle trees close to the small hut. Eric thought that the terrorists must think that if the vehicles were under the trees, then satellites could not detect them. Apparently, the terrorists were not aware that the most advanced Israeli satellites could also detect heat signatures and anomalies on the ground such as a vehicle under a tree. But no, his instinct told him they were left there on purpose to lure them here. Moreover, Eric thought there were too many vehicles in this area for one small hut. The hut must be an entrance to something bigger underground. Eric gave the order to search the area to check for booby traps and hidden cameras. They found the front door of the hut booby-trapped with electric wires attached to the handle, which when pulled would have electrocuted the person and set off an explosion. The two security cameras on either side of the clearing were disabled by them as well. They also found four large air vents and a large hidden escape exit door seemingly unguarded about 1,000 feet away from the hut entrance at the other end of the clearing. This would be their entry point. The satellite above was tracking any approaching men or vehicles. So far none, except for a large camp of armed men less than three miles away. However, satellites showed no unusual movement in the camp. Above ground the place seemed almost deserted. Eric thought that it was too quiet and the unguarded exit door too obvious.

Even though Eric sensed this was a trap, he knew he had to spring it himself to get Al Kaduna. Eric called his team commandos on his comm link to stake out the perimeter of the clearing while he alone entered the non-booby-trapped exit door at the rear of the clearing. He told them that he would keep in touch with them as he explored what was on the other side of the door. But due to the danger below, he gave orders that they should not follow him unless ordered to do so. Ordinarily, as the group leader, he would have designated this function, but he wanted Al Kaduna to himself. When he opened the metal door, he saw steps leading down to a completely dark interior. He simply turned on the black light attached to his army helmet which allowed him to clearly see in the dark. He quickly but cautiously started to descend and explore the interior. At the bottom of the stairs, he found that there were eight rooms, one filled with communications equipment and one with ammunition and machine guns. He now realized that something was blocking his comm link signals to his men when he tried to call to check in, but he had no time to stop and figure it out. More importantly, his men were also unable to contact him to alert him that almost immediately after he descended into the underground complex, the nearby terrorist army had mobilized and was quickly heading towards them. Ignorant of the new danger, Eric continued to explore the dark underground hideout. The most intriguing items he found in a room were four American

VAMPIRE missiles stacked in the corner. Each cost over one million dollars and was highly classified and dangerous. VAMPIRE was an acronym for "Vehicle Agnostic Modular Palletized ISR Rocket Equipment" and could be used to turn most moving vehicles into mobile laser rocket launchers. Eric thought, *How did these American missiles get here? And where is Al Kaduna and the other terrorists?* Before he left this room, he took photos of the serial numbers and ID markings on each of the four VAMPIRE missiles for future research on the origins of the missiles. The room was also filled almost to the ceiling with boxes of high-powered ammunition and explosives as well.

As he slowly opened the door to the next room in the underground complex, he curiously focused on six buckets lined up close to the rear wall lit up by his helmet light. They were filled to the top with what seemed like black rocks. He really didn't know what he was looking at except that the rocks were sorted according to size from smallest to largest. Each bucket next to the other contained larger and larger rocks. On top of the bucket with the largest rocks was the largest one about the size of a bumpy half-pound potato with a sort of grayish black color. As he was standing in the middle of the room puzzling and concentrating for a moment about these strange rocks, he was tackled from the side with the force of a bulldozer. It was Mohammed Al Kaduna. The unexpected tackle by the huge African giant of a man knocked Eric clear across the room, making him lose his rifle, helmet, and pistol as he hit the wall. Eric, quickly regaining his balance, was surprised to see that Al Kaduna, instead of following up his initial attack, walked slowly and confidently to the door, locked it, and flipped on the light switch. He then turned to face Eric.

Almost snarling, he said to Eric in Arabic, "This is a trap, you stupid fool, that you didn't catch. I called my army from a section of the complex where telecommunication signals are not blocked to begin the attack on your people above ground the moment I heard you enter through the rear door which I left unguarded on purpose. I knew you would come for me as soon as I let myself be seen by satellite." He had waited for Eric in this terrorist underground command center with the patience of a leopard in tree waiting to pounce on its prey. He continued, "The rest of my army will be here very soon to kill your comrades above us, but I wanted you to myself— alone, to finish some unfinished business. I'm going to fuck your white ass now, even if I have to fuck your dead corpse!" He continued to taunt Eric as the two men circled each other like caged beasts. Al Kaduna continued taunting him, saying that Eric was so pretty but so stupid for not knowing that he had been looking at the buckets filled with uncut diamonds that made him richer than Eric could ever hope to be. Licking his lips, he told Eric, "How sweet your ass will feel when I finally take my turn to put my big cock up your asshole with you helpless to stop me."

While Al Kaduna continued to taunt him, Eric said nothing, just continued to size up with cold calculation the giant beast of a man circling before him. It is said that humans are the most dangerous animals on Earth. And these two were about to prove it. Eric's extreme military training against Al Kaduna's honed animal-like instincts with almost the size and strength of a gorilla. Adding to Eric's repulsion was Al Kaduna's smell in this small airless room. He stank like a man who hadn't washed or bathed in days or weeks. Eric's dense, well-trained muscles of steel tensed, ready for anything.

Finally, Al Kaduna laughed loudly, "I really enjoyed surprising you."

Eric forcefully replied in Arabic, "I am not surprised to find a cowardly, rabid animal like you in a pit like this!"

When Al Kaduna heard the word "animal," without giving Eric another moment to think, Al Kaduna took out a six inch, razor-sharp steel blade and sprang at him. Both men knew it would be a fight to the death. At the last second, Eric sidestepped the onslaught, but Al Kaduna's huge hand caught him, throwing Eric to the floor and pinning Eric down underneath him before Eric could unsheathe his own blade. Al Kaduna's huge, muscled body weighing more than 250 pounds now lay on top of Eric, helping him press his blade held by his two powerful hands into Eric's chest. Al Kaduna's face was close enough to Eric's face that Eric could smell his disgusting, putrid breath. But he did not let it distract him. Slowly, Eric pushed against Al Kaduna's hands holding the blade above him, lifting him away with his own steel-like muscled grip but not before Al Kaduna made a cut through Eric's uniform, leaving a bloodless red mark across Eric's chest. Both men knew it was a life and death moment.

Just then the locked door burst open. It was Sergeant Isaac Caveda. He had disobeyed Eric's order to remain outside above ground because he had sensed something was wrong. Eric had not been calling to check in. He had come to rescue his friend and military comrade. He instantly shot Al Kaduna in the side of his torso, which caused him to slump over Eric, pinning Eric under him while releasing pressure on the deadly blade. Isaac ran to Eric to push off Al Kaduna's body. But the murdering terrorist was faking death. As Isaac touched Al Kaduna's body, Al Kaduna quickly stood up, and with the same movement, he swung his blade around, deeply cutting Isaac's throat with it. This caused Isaac to fall backwards on top of the buckets of uncut diamonds, scattering the diamonds across the floor, his throat wound gushing blood everywhere, covering the diamonds on the floor and proving they were truly blood diamonds now!

This interruption gave Eric the chance he needed. Hurled by Isaac's fall on to the buckets of diamonds, the largest uncut diamond skidded and rolled across the floor within Eric's reach. He grabbed it, made a fist, clenching the huge uncut diamond, then jumped to his feet, swung around with the full force of his own muscled body, and smashed it and his clenched steel fist against Al Kaduna's jaw. By its cracking sound, Eric could tell he had broken Al Kaduna's jaw. But it only made his huge opponent stagger back one step. In the next moment, Eric dropped the diamond and unsheathed his own huge, steel-bladed knife from his knife holster belt. Before Al Kaduna could regain his balance, Eric lunged at him, thrusting his blade up through Al Kaduna's stomach, missing his bony rib cage to puncture the heart. It was a technique used by the ancient Romans in close hand-to-hand battles that Eric had studied. It was supposed to incur instant death in an adversary. Eric was glad to discover that it worked. But not before he firmly said into Al Kaduna's ear, up close and personal, "How do you like my nine inches?"

Al Kaduna's facial expression was one of complete horror as Eric twisted his nine inch blade to open a gaping hole in his enemy's gut. Al Kaduna's hot blood gushed everywhere, drenching Eric. It was a mortal wound and they both knew it. The last thing Al Kaduna saw was Eric's smiling face as his opponent's dead body crumpled to the floor at Eric's feet. As this happened Eric thought, *Vengeance served hot or cold balances the scales and feels so good. Better than a hundred therapy sessions!* Furthermore, he told himself, he had just made sure that no more innocent people would ever be raped and murdered by this monster. Eric was surprised that he felt so satisfied. He quickly stepped over his enemy's bloody dead body to get to his fellow commando and friend, Isaac.

Eric took one look at Isaac holding his neck, trying to stop the blood, and knew Isaac's neck wound was fatal. He knelt down by his friend, helping Isaac keep pressure on his wound and said, "My friend, thank you for saving my life. Can I do anything for you?" He knew Isaac was desperately in love with him, but Eric had never encouraged it.

Isaac looked up at his unreachable love and softly asked, "Kiss me." Eric immediately bent over and kissed Isaac on his lips. Isaac died smiling, looking up at Eric. As Eric breathed a sad sigh, he closed Isaac's eyes. He then took a minute to say the Jewish prayer for the dead over his friend.

It was now time to think of the living. Eric put Isaac's body over his shoulder as gently as he could and carried his friend from this blood soaked room, stopping only to collect their weapons and equipment. He then headed up the stairs of the underground terrorist complex and into the sunlight. As he climbed the stairs, Eric realized he was at peace with himself again. He felt that his PTSD was completely healed. But as he opened the door at the top of the stairs, it wasn't a peaceful scene he encountered in the jungle clearing outside. The Israeli commandos were under attack and engaging in a full-blown firefight with the heavily armed two hundred plus soldier terrorist army that had just arrived. Al Kaduna's trap had been sprung as they encircled and attacked the Israeli commandos or so the terrorists thought.

Eric quickly used his comm link to contact Sam on board Dragonfly to say, "The squad is under attack, and we need help fast!"

Sam responded, "I have been monitoring the situation. The minute you entered the underground complex, the terrorists started to mobilize, but I couldn't get through to you because your comm link was down. However, we are ready to engage. I was only waiting to hear from you." Sam quickly ended the call, turned to the two pilots and said, "We understand that orders from the High Command dictate that we do not engage under any circumstances unless Israeli lives are at risk. This qualifies! The lives of our fellow soldiers are at risk. But I have one question, we are not going to blow ourselves up along with half of Africa?"

Captain Gil Sofer, the senior pilot, calmly replied, "I have been with the development of *Dragonfly* since the very beginning, and I strongly believe that the operational constraints placed on her are only political. *Dragonfly* is ready for a real world battle test."

Sam took a deep breath and said, "Therefore, by my command, engage! Let's see what this baby can do!"

Sofer told Colonel Reichman, "Sit down, strap in, and watch what this fully operational aerial battleship can do. And find out why my nickname for our ship is not *Dragonfly* but *Dragon Fire*!" Surprised, Sam noted to himself that Gil did not use the word helicopter.

Next the senior pilot turned to Lieutenant Elon Dagen, the copilot, and said, "Fusion drive engaged. Force field laser shields up! We're going to war!"

The copilot cooly replied, "Roger! All systems operational and armed." He then quickly turned to Colonel Reichman and said with a wry half smile, "You're now going to discover the truth. This ain't no helicopter!" *Dragonfly* emerged from its silent hiding place above the billowy jungle clouds, with its outside skin glowing with pulsating laser light rings running back and forth against its silver exterior with all weapons systems armed and fully operational. Its pulsating, glowing laser light rings could now be seen by half the country below. The pilots immediately fired a laser to establish a protective perimeter shield almost as hot as the sun itself, but as thin as a wafer in the shape of a dome six stories tall around the now surrounded Israeli commandos. This stopped the firefight cold. No weapon could breach that shield from either side. The Israelis were all pleased to discover it was impenetrable to any existing armaments since a laser shield like this had never been tested before in actual battle.

However, the terrorists now turned their considerable firepower away from the commandos and towards *Dragonfly*. The terrorist army fired rounds of rockets from two armored rocket launcher vehicles as well as everything else they had, including rocket grenade launchers and machine guns firing armor-piercing bullets. All the crew of *Dragonfly* felt were mild bumps as the rockets and bullets hit *Dragonfly's* laser shield protecting the ship and were instantly disintegrated. In fact, all this terrorist firepower impact accomplished was to get the two pilots' attention. While still maintaining the protective laser shield around the Israeli Special Forces, the senior pilot turned the aerial battleship and faced its attackers. It instantly fired its white hot lasers, creating a pulsating wall of laser light behind all the terrorists. When it did this, the terrorists thought it had misfired its weapons. But no, the pilots were establishing the rear wall of a laser cage to make sure no one escaped. The senior pilot now aimed *Dragonfly's* front lasers at the two rocket launcher vehicles, configured his control panel to pinpoint accuracy, and simultaneously fired two beams of lethal laser light. They instantly disintegrated them, killing the terrorist crews and turning the two vehicles and rockets into unusable, smoldering metal. Quickly reconfiguring their control panel and adjusting the spread of its lasers to a wider spread, about 150 feet, the pilots then proceeded to track and incinerate the rest of the two hundred plus armed terrorist soldiers.

Or as the copilot, Elon Dagen, told Colonel Reichman, "It's time to mow the lawn."

As the laser light beam moved across the battlefield, everything it touched evaporated into a small cloud of black smoke—nothing remained—no bodies, no clothes, no weapons—nothing. The operation took less than three minutes to completely "neutralize" the entire heavily armed terrorist army. In those three minutes, the future of warfare changed as the Israeli commando team glimpsed what warfare would look like at the end of the twenty-first and into the twenty-second century.

After the pilots on *Dragonfly* made sure the area was cleared of terrorists by using heat sensor technology to scour the surrounding dense jungle and road for any human heat signatures, which only took another two minutes, they lowered the protective dome laser shield around the Israeli's Special Forces and gently landed the aerial battleship in the middle of the jungle clearing close to the commandos.

As the returning Israeli Special Force soldiers climbed aboard their aerial battleship, Sam's heart sank when he saw Eric carrying Isaac's dead body. The whole team was saddened at this sight, but Eric wouldn't let anyone else help him. Due to Eric's enormous strength, he was able to lift both himself and Isaac on board at the same time. As he carefully laid Isaac's body on the floor of the arial battleship, he looked up at Sam and said, "Isaac died a hero saving me." Sam replied that he would make sure Isaac was given a funeral with full military honors and the Medal of Valor, the highest military award Israel can give to a soldier.

Next Eric motioned to Sam to follow him to where the pilots sat as the rest of the team strapped themselves in for the return flight. Eric asked the pilots if *Dragonfly* had the power to eliminate the underground terrorist complex. He explained that it was full of highly sophisticated communications equipment, armaments, rockets, and enough uncut blood diamonds to fund terrorism in Africa for years. He added it was about twenty feet below the ground.

The pilots looked at each other as Gil Sofer, the senior pilot replied, "To clarify, you want an empty hole in the ground twenty feet deep where the underground complex is now?"

Eric nodded. "Yes, but I don't want any of the native flora and fauna damaged when we do it. And one more thing, the blow back from the explosions of the rockets and munitions stored there could damage *Dragonfly* if we are too close."

The pilots looked at each other again for assurance before the senior pilot told them, "Give us a minute to configure our screens to the bunker's outline." After a minute, he continued, "We are now engaging the fusion anti-gravity device to take her up five miles, not so much because we are scared of the explosion blowback once our shields are up, but we want to test the lasers at that range." Both Sam and Eric nodded their heads in agreement, in effect giving the pilots permission to proceed. When they very quickly reached that height, the senior pilot turned to them and said, "As requested, there will be a twenty foot deep hole in the ground configured to the exact outline of the complex—not an inch more. All we need now is an order."

So, Sam said, "By my command, destroy the terrorist underground complex."

When the pilot pressed a button on his control panel, a beam of white hot laser light shot into the ground below. Seconds later, Gil Sofer looked up and said, "Mission accomplished!" As predicted, they all thought they heard distant muffled explosions from the munitions stored below them. They also discovered that the deadly laser weapon worked perfectly at that range. Moreover, Gil Sofer thought it had not yet reached its maximum range. In the years that follow, Gil, along with his copilot, Elon Dagen, would become senior instructors and department heads on aerial laser technology and warfare at Israel's Technion Institute, establishing a new department for it. Legends in their own right. But for now, they were marking new trails in military warfare.

Dragonfly darted down, hovering above the new hole in the jungle floor to review the laser weapon's effectiveness. The new hole in the ground was indeed configured exactly to the outline of the underground complex.

Elon Dagen commented, "I think that if we return in a year, this new hole will probably turn into a jungle watering hole for animals."

However, what was not noticed by the crew of *Dragonfly*, in spite of everything nearby being completely disintegrated, was the hundreds of still perfectly good uncut diamonds lying on the dirt floor of the new hole that would soon be covered by collapsing mud walls. So, the crew did not notice the most important discovery in front of them—that a searing laser blast had no effect on diamond crystals. Uncut diamond crystals when hit by a laser only refract the laser light into dozens of different, beautiful, and harmless colors of the light spectrum. In fact, it took another decade for Gil and Elon to discover that only when certain diamonds are cut in a certain way, they reflect laser light directly back to the point of origin, making possible very effective defensive weapons against laser weaponry and the very destructive wars of the future.

But for now, it took a little more than one hour at supersonic Mach 2 cruising speed to arrive back at the secret Israeli airfare base in the Negev. Mission accomplished, the most wanted terrorist in Africa was terminated! And the whole operation had taken a little less than the planned six hours due to the extraordinary speed and weapon capability of Israel's new aerial battleship nicknamed *Dragonfly*. But after watching *Dragonfly* in action during the battle, all the commandos and pilots agreed to give their battleship a new name. Its name was now *Dragon Fire*!

CHAPTER SIX

HOME SWEET HOME

Two days later in the afternoon behind a closed door meeting at the headquarters of the Mossad in Tel Aviv after the Special Forces team had returned, the prime minister was furious at Shimon Weisman, the defense secretary, who was looking at Alon Reuben, the Director of Mossad, with knives in his eyes. Major General Chiam Savage, in charge of Sayeret Matkal, was in the meeting too, looking up at the ceiling, trying to ignore it all.

The prime minister continued, "What does the word covert mean? I will tell you all what it means. It means hidden or secret! Apparently, our Israeli satellite watching the simple tactical test exercise by our aerial battleship to determine its long range flying abilities authorized by myself was joined by American, Russian, Chinese, and British satellites all watching the same exercise turn into a full scale battle with the largest terrorist army in Africa. A battle in which our aerial battleship obliterated the opposing side within minutes. And now I have to deal with a political shit storm."

Everyone in the room agreed that even though the mission goal had been accomplished, it came at the cost of revealing Israel's technological prowess to the world. Technologies like those used by Israel's laser aerial battleship were supposed to be theoretical at this time; certainly not built yet and definitely not functionally tested under real battle conditions. It was more than a twenty year technological jump in warfare. Every major power could see the advantage and wanted a piece!

Finally, Major General Chiam Savage joined the conversation, saying, "In my opinion, not only did our aerial battleship meet all its goals in actual battle but exceeded them. Because of this, Israel needs a whole fleet of them."

The PM turned to everyone in the room and asked, "Just where are we going to get an extra billion dollars to build this fleet?" No one answered.

Also in the room, sitting and listening at the other end of the table, was Jacob Kurtz. Jacob noted that the PM's criticism did not sit well with anyone in the room. He thought the PM's criticism was shortsighted, bordering on stupidity. So, he interjected, "We can't do anything about the world knowing the abilities of our new aerial battleship so let's change the narrative. Spin it like Israel wants the world to know it. Make heroes of the Special Forces team. I'll handle the promotion and media end of the story. Moreover, I think each aerial battleship, in my estimation, is worth at least ten thousand additional soldiers on the battlefield and we should not call it a helicopter anymore. I'm very proud at what the Special Forces team has just accomplished. Oh, and I almost forgot, the new nickname our military is now calling our battleship is *Dragon Fire* not *Dragonfly*. I like that name better so I will introduce it to the world by its new name." Lastly, to lighten the mood, he added, "Don't forget I'm having a party tonight and I'm looking forward to seeing you all and your wives at my place."

Everyone there agreed with the positive spin Jacob was suggesting. Unbeknown to them, it also fit well with the political agenda he had developed for Eric. The meeting ended soon after that. As Jacob Kurtz left the meeting, he realized that yet again the prime minister was over his head in solving even a minor crisis. However, Jacob was always ready to help for the good of the country.

Two days earlier, Jacob had walked into his living room after dinner and announced to Mark and Alisa, "Eric and Sam are back safe in Israel and Mohammed Al Kaduna has been killed along with many other terrorists. They both should be home either late tonight or first thing in the morning. In any case, it's time for you to leave. But all of you are invited to a dinner party I am having here two nights from now."

Jacob had Noah drive Alisa home while Mark walked down the hill, anxiously anticipating Eric's arrival. When he arrived home, he was very thankful that someone, probably Noah since he had access via a biometric security entrance key, had cleaned up after the party and put any salvageable food in the refrigerator. Moreover, Mark had discovered that his friend Jacob was much more complex than he had previously guessed, but he couldn't put his finger on the whole truth of it yet.

Eric opened the front door of their house about 9:00 a.m. the next morning. He needed to spend the previous night on the base to clean up, get debriefed, and rest. Arriving home covered in blood and smelling like a swamp would not have been received well. The long hot shower he had taken at the base had also washed the dark brown dye from his hair. Additionally, Eric thought it was time to get rid of his beard. But most importantly, Eric used the time to get control and bury his black side before he saw Mark. That is what Mark had called it when he sensed it in him. They only emotion he could not control was his deep sadness at losing Isaac. Eric, moreover, surprised himself this time about how deeply he enjoyed killing

Al Kaduna. Yes, Eric knew he was a natural born killer, a facility that had served him well in the Mossad and Sayeret Matkal. But he would never let Mark know the dirty details. In fact, Eric was a little apprehensive about revealing to Mark the full extent of his missions. Not only because it would violate national security, but it might alter Mark's love and acceptance of him. In spite of that, Eric smiled inwardly to himself as he walked towards his house, thinking as he approached that the military actually trained him to do a better job at what he loved; hunting and killing, but without penalty or repercussion while rewarding him for it.

He entered his house, blond, clean shaven, and movie star handsome, just like when he first met Mark except with a few recent cuts and bruises especially on his knuckles. Mark took one look at him and flew into his arms. They both stood hugging each other for a long while, saying nothing, emotionally decompressing. Before Mark could say anything, Eric said, "That's it. I am never going on one of these missions again. I swear to you. And I am very sorry about our dinner party." Then Eric just smiled at Mark.

In that instant, Mark realized that Eric's demons had vanished, and Eric was his old self again. There would be no more need for any more PTSD therapy sessions. A deep joy of life bathed both of them.

Eric knew that Mark's love always helped heal him and banish his black side. The first thing Eric always noticed about his husband was his sexy shaved head and wonderful hairy chest. Then, almost at the same time, Eric was enveloped in Mark's body scent. Mark always used a bath and shower wash called Coriander made by the famous soap and lotion manufacturer Kiehl. It smelled slightly like a mixture of citrus and rosewood. It was always an enormous turn on for Eric and so different from the hell pit he had just survived. Even though Eric was almost a head taller and bigger than Mark, Eric always felt himself more than just safe but a complete person when with him.

Eric now told Mark about something that Mark could sense was very important to him. Eric wanted to attend Isaac Caveda's family funeral tomorrow along with all of Isaac's military comrades and their spouses, who were invited too. Sam and Alisa would be there as well. So, he wanted Mark to attend with him. He told Mark, "Isaac died saving my life," but added no more details than that.

Mark immediately replied that he would be honored to attend and was also thankful that Isaac had saved his partner's life. Moreover, Mark had learned not to ask any more questions about this startling news because he would not get any more information from Eric. He was actually surprised he was told this much and very curious about the funeral that they would attend tomorrow.

Eric then nonchalantly added, "I almost forgot, but I brought a present back from the mission for you." Mark was really surprised and delighted when he heard this because Eric had never before done anything like it. Eric told Mark, "Just hold out your hand." He reached into his pocket and placed a grayish black rock into the palm of Mark's hand.

Mark's smile turned to a questioning look as he studied this rock that weighed nearly a half a pound and was in the shape of a bumpy potato. Mark's unenthusiastic but very diplomatic response was, "This will make a nice paperweight on my desk. Thank you very much for thinking of me and bringing me this rock as a gift."

Eric smiled his big Hollywood film star smile, almost laughing, when he said, "I thought you were smart enough to recognize an uncut diamond when you saw one."

As Mark walked over to a well-lit table and placed the rock on it, he noticed that sections of his rock looked like crystal showing through its surface. Mark instantly realized his mistake. So, he quickly turned back to Eric and told him, "Come over here, you big blond hunk, because this daddy is going to thank you like it's a real diamond!"

Eric immediately blushed, lowered his gaze, and took a step forward. He loved it when Mark turned the aggressor in their relationship.

And Mark loved it when Eric's dense muscles of steel turned supple as Mark complimented him on how silky soft his skin felt covering his rock hard muscles while pressing against Eric's hairless washboard abs and chest. But what Mark didn't know and was about to happily discover was that Eric's recent successful fight to the death with his archenemy had made Eric extraordinarily horny. Two hours later, they lay exhausted in each other's arms from making love. Eric said he wanted to stay home the remainder of the day and swim some laps. Mark had no problem having his partner all to himself. They both felt it was good to be home together.

Later, Mark casually mentioned to Eric that Jacob was having a dinner party at his house day after tomorrow and they were invited. Eric immediately asked if the prime minister was invited?

Mark replied, "Probably, they are friends."

At the mention that the PM was going to be there, Eric tensed as his political antenna started to vibrate. When Mark sensed Eric tense, then he too realized he needed to be "on guard" at the party.

Early the next morning, Eric drove them to the funeral in Eric's army green Land Rover Defender 90X. Mark could still see how enjoyable it was for Eric to drive his big Land Rover that Eric had received when they had exchanged new cars as wedding gifts for each other. It was still Eric's toy. While being driven there, Mark couldn't help but feel a bit insecure or even jealous of Isaac's relationship with Eric. It was a part of Eric's life that he was only vaguely allowed to see. But Mark knew it was time to be generous of spirit and to support his partner. And that was what he intended to do as he dismissed all negative thoughts from his mind. When they arrived at the family funeral, it was already crowded with Isaac's Special Forces comrades and spouses. Isaac's family had insisted on a family funeral in the tradition of Beta Israel, not a military funeral. It was being held in a small synagogue inland in a small village near Be'er Sheva. The solemn, short funeral ceremony was conducted by a Beta Israel priest called a *kohanin*. Isaac's body had been wrapped in a white sheet and placed in a plain wooden coffin. The family was holding the ceremony early the next day after they had received Isaac's body from the military. As is the custom with all Jewish funerals, the body is buried almost immediately or as soon as possible.

In fact, as far as Mark could discern with his non-religious background, the burial customs of the Beta Israel and mainstream Jewish community were very similar. However, there was one interesting custom that caught Mark's eye. Everyone was asked to wash their hands upon leaving. Eric explained that this ancient custom was supposed to wash away any death demons that had been around the body. After the funeral, Mark also overheard Colonel Sam Reichman officially tell Isaac's parents that the IDF, together with the Israeli Special Forces, would hold an additional ceremony in one month's time to give the Israeli Medal of Valor, Israel's highest military honor, posthumously, to Sergeant Isaac Caveda. What made Mark uncomfortable, though, as they left the funeral, was that Eric teared up when he hugged Isaac's mother and father. It raised questions again in Mark's mind about how close these two guys really were. There was no party afterwards, so everyone went home. Eric didn't say anything all the way home. Mark thought it was a good idea to give Eric as much emotional space as he needed. Not much was said for the rest of the day or at dinner either.

In the morning of Jacob's party after a good night's sleep, Mark turned to Eric and said, "I have been thinking about the uncut diamond. I'm not stupid. I know it came from Africa and is probably a blood diamond. That means that many children probably died mining it. And we both know that when cut and polished a stone like that will be worth millions. So, since we don't need the money, I would like to sell your present and donate the proceeds to an Israeli charity I know. One that takes care of special needs children of all faiths; children that no one wants or knows how to care for, if it's okay with you?"

Eric, nodding in agreement, took Mark's head in his big hands to hold it while he kissed him hard on the lips. All he said was, "Did you know that I am yours forever?"

Mark, looking Eric straight in the eyes, softly replied, "I know."

CHAPTER SEVEN

THE COLONEL

Jacob's party as usual was a glittering affair. Half the political and financial elites of Israel were there. The valet parked cars extended all the way down the hill passed Mark and Eric's front door. So, they decided to walk, arriving a little late. When Major Eric Jansen walked into the party, everyone turned and clapped. Jacob Kurtz's media blitz celebrating the successful assassination of the terrorist who had kidnapped the bus load of Israeli tourists in Egypt was already in gear. The newspapers, TV, and streaming services were full of the story. Eric instinctively raised both hands with his two figures in a *V* shape for victory while flashing his movie star smile. The guests went wild in applause, calling Eric's name. Mark took a step back, giving Eric his moment but also observing the audience. He noticed that the only two people in the crowded room that were not wildly applauding were Jacob Kurtz who was, like himself, cooly observing the scene, and the prime minister, who tried not to show his annoyance at

Eric's popularity. Mark astutely observed that the PM correctly sensed a political rival in Eric.

Both Eric and Mark spent most of the evening enjoying the party. Eric used it to network politically while Mark reconnected with his old treasure hunting teammates and friends, Ariel and Julie Kurtz, Sam and Alisa Reichman, Solomon Levine, and even Dr. Nikol Yoram was there. Based on rumors as well as Mark dropping heavy hints, they were all eager to hear about the location of the hidden Temple treasure mentioned in the Copper Scroll Mark had discovered. But Mark was not yet ready to reveal its secret.

Later, as some of the guests started to leave, Mark overheard the name *Dragon Fire* as he walked past a group of men speaking quietly together. He recognized the men as Shimon Weisman, the defense minister, Alon Reuben, the director of the Mossad, and Chiam Savage, the major general in charge of the Sayeret Matkal, the prime minister, and lastly their host, Jacob Kurtz. So, Mark turned and casually said hello. Seeing Mark approach this group, Eric and Sam also quickly walked over to be part of it. They were always a little uneasy about what Mark might say to the PM and wanted to be close, in case they needed to do damage control. Shimon Weisman, the defense minister, asked Mark how he was enjoying the party.

Mark replied, "It is a splendid party, and I even used the front door to get in this time!" Everyone chuckled at this, including Sam, but not Eric who knew nothing about Mark's embarrassing fence climbing episode that had taken place while Eric was in Africa. Mark turned to Eric, who had a questioning look on his face, and said, "I will tell you about it later, maybe. Not my finest hour!"

As the group continued to talk, Mark asked, "What does the name *Dragon Fire* mean?" He had been too busy to read the newspapers or listen to the TV recently.

Major General Chiam Savage explained to Mark, "It is an aerial battleship whose technology is beyond the most advanced helicopter and can hover or actually float without wings, fly faster than the speed of sound, and fire laser weapons powered by a fusion reaction that are the most formidable in the world. Moreover, Israel is the only country in the world that has one and it is one of the main reasons why Eric and the entire Special Force team except for Sergeant Reuben returned so quickly and safely from their latest mission." Eric nodded in agreement when the major general said this. The major general quickly added, "I haven't said anything that wasn't recently splashed all over the world media."

Mark replied, "Well, then, the *Dragon Fire* aerial battleship sounds great. It doesn't sound like Israel has a problem."

Next, the prime minister added, "There is no problem except for the immense funding necessary to build a whole fleet of them. We need at least a billion dollars to fund the next stage and we don't have it unless we want to develop it jointly with another country, which means sharing our secret technology."

Mark thought for a second and said, "I have a hunch how to find the money." As soon as Jacob heard Mark say the word "hunch," Jacob interrupted the conversation and told them they all needed to move this discussion into his office before another word was said. Jacob knew that Mark's hunches had previously led to the discovery of two immense treasures in Israel and realized his living room filled with party guests was too public for such a subject.

As soon as everyone was seated and settled in Jacob's office, Jacob asked Mark to please continue. So, Mark explained to everyone in the room, "Eric and I have unlocked the secret of the Copper Scroll, which is truly a legitimate treasure map to the Temple treasure if you know how to read it and not just a ruse to confuse the Roman conquerors."

Eric interjected, "It was really Mark who found the key to the treasure not me."

To which Mark replied, "I could not have done it without Eric's superb linguistic ability deciphering key words."

Mark continued to explain, "Many people have tried to use the Copper Scroll to find the Temple treasure, but none have succeeded. Thus, the general consensus thought the scroll was created to misdirect the Roman conquerors when it was found in Israel hidden amongst the famous Dead Sea Scrolls written on parchment. It points to sixty-three specific locations of hidden gold with many of the locations still existing today, but no gold was ever found. When the Romans looted the Jerusalem Temple in 70 CE, they took away a fortune in gold, enough to build the Coliseum still standing in Rome today and many other monuments that have since been destroyed. The chronicles of the day stated that the treasure storerooms of the Temple were completely full when the Romans looted and then destroyed them. So therefore, the Romans looted all the gold that was there. Right? Wrong! The key word is "full." The huge treasure storerooms on the Temple Mount had been full for years with more and more gold pouring in every year. So actually, the Temple priests started hiding and storing the Temple gold offsite decades before the Roman conquest." Mark took a breath to read the room to make sure they were all following his explanation before he continued. "Thus, it is my hunch that the priests were actually equally scared of the rapacious kings of Judea looting Temple gold years before the Roman conquest. So, I believe, that almost as soon as the Temple treasury was built, the priests had the problem of safely storing their treasure. According to Flavius Josephus, the first century eyewitness and chronicler to the siege and destruction of Jerusalem, the Temple storerooms were huge and filled to overflowing with gold and silver when the Romans sacked it. Therefore, my hunch is that the storerooms were just too small to hold all of it. I am basing this on the fact that according to modern estimates the population of the Roman Empire at its height was approximately twenty million people. Historians estimate that 10 percent or about two million people were Jewish. Every male Jew above the age of twenty was taxed a half shekel annually for the upkeep of the Temple." According to Mark's analysis, this would have been more than enough for the annual upkeep of the Temple. "However, the overflow treasury storage problem occurred because of the additional tithe system that every male Jew was supposed to donate annually to the Temple by religious law. This 'tithing' or giving ten percent of your income occurred every year. So again, according to Flavius Josephus, most wealthy Jews strictly followed this religious practice. This money was supposed to help rebuild the Temple but still kept pouring in annually after the Temple had been rebuilt. So yes, the

Temple treasury was full when it was sacked by the Romans, but the Romans didn't get all of it by a long shot and they killed the priests who knew the secret!"

Mark further explained, "My eureka moment came when I was looking at photos of the back side of the scroll and noticed pinprick holes in the copper. Then I looked at photos of the scroll's frontside and I noticed that these pinholes are in the center of a name of a town or village. I already knew that some of these locations had been unsuccessfully explored for treasure. So, therefore, on a hunch, I started connecting the locations of the pinholes by drawing lines between them, emanating from Jerusalem as the starting point." He continued to explain, "To check my theory, I drove to a field where these lines on the scroll supposedly crossed. There, I noticed the lines on the map represented low-rise stone walls. On closer inspection of these walls, I noticed that one of the precisely cut stone blocks had cracked over the years. Probing with my figures and looking closely inside the crack, I rubbed the inside of the hole with my handkerchief. That's when I saw the unmistakable shine that I know well—gold! At that moment, I further concluded that the connecting lines on the Copper Scroll represented walls that were constructed with hollow stone building blocks of various sizes filled with gold! So, to the outside world, it looked like the ancient temple priests never ended their rebuilding and maintenance program of the Jerusalem Holy Temple. But actually, they were hollowing out and pouring molten gold inside stone blocks, then sealing the hole with a stone plug. They, then, built low-rise stone walls transversing Israel like a spiderweb while hiding the gold in plain sight! Of the sixty-three locations mentioned on the front of the scroll indicating hidden gold, about half have a pinhole in the copper visible on the reverse side. Thus, the locations with the pinhole are the locations where the gold filled stone walls connect. So, all we need to do is find the stone walls with the gold filled stone blocks, break them open with a hammer, and voila, you will have your extra billion dollars you need to further develop the *Dragon Fire* project."

The group went dead silent processing when Mark finished explaining his hunch. The prime minister was first to speak when he said, "I don't believe any of it."

Jacob sat forward in his chair and said to the group, "It's easy enough to prove. Let's find a wall and split open some rocks."

Mark nodded his head in agreement. Further, Mark added, "One of the walls that should have the gold filled stone blocks is located very close to where we are standing now! So, who wants to hunt Temple treasure by moonlight with me tonight?" Eric and Sam raised their hands first, then Jacob, and then the whole group.

The PM said, "But I'm wearing a new pair of shoes not appropriate for archeological digs."

Mark retorted, "If we don't find anything, I will buy you a new pair of shoes!" This sealed the deal. Next Eric asked Jacob how many flashlights and hammers did he have on hand? The enthusiasm in the group was palpable. Jacob's sophisticated adult party had turned into a fun party atmosphere of a boy's night out!

Before Jacob left to find the equipment, the defense minister told everyone, "Please wait a minute. Major General Chiam Savage and I want to make an announcement. Major Eric Jansen has been promoted to full colonel, retired, in the Israeli Special Forces, skipping the rank of lieutenant colonel for his great services to Israel." Everyone clapped and congratulated Eric, including Jacob before he disappeared to find flashlights and hammers. The excitement of his new military promotion added to the excitement of the night's treasure hunt!

Between the bodyguards and parking attendants, they gathered enough extra flashlights for everyone in the group. But Jacob was only able to find two hammers from his own utility closet. They told their surprised wives to wait for them at the party, saying they would return soon.

Mark took the lead in the group, including some of the most powerful men in Israel's military/industrial complex, as they scampered off into the dark like a group of mischievous teenage boys. The time was early December, and the evening air was brisk and the sky clear and filled with stars —a perfect night for a treasure hunt! About a quarter of a mile down the hill going south towards Jerusalem, they came upon a low-rise wall about four feet high running along a flat plain. It was basically a heap of rocks that stretched into the night. Mark said, "I am sure this is the wall for which we are looking."

Sam added, "If Mark is correct, then we should all start removing these loose rocks on top to see what's underneath." Everyone helped by lifting and gently putting the top rocks aside to uncover underneath a smaller wall made of two levels of finely cut intact stone blocks laid precisely on top of one another. They all agreed that it looked like the rocks covering the cut stone wall had been put there on purpose to hide the smaller wall. It was made to look like a taller, crumbling old stone wall had collapsed on itself hiding the bottom stone blocks.

With all the flashlights shining on the exposed part of the stone wall, Eric and Sam volunteered to hammer one stone block. After several blows to the top side of the stone block, it cracked open revealing something else solid inside. It was too dusty and dark to determine what it was. So, the PM asked them to chip away the rest of the outside block of stone.

It did not take much more hammering before a different kind of rock appeared. It was heavier and denser than the surrounding limestone. As he lifted this new rock from its recently encased space, the major general spit on it and wiped it off with his handkerchief, saying at the same time that he thought it weighed about three pounds. The shine of gold instantly gleamed against the flashlights focused on it.

Upon seeing the gleam of gold, Mark yelled "Eureka! We found the gold!" His voice echoed over the surrounding plains and hills. Everyone was stunned by the discovery as if they really didn't believe they were going to discover anything important. But they did!

Jacob immediately put his hand over Mark's mouth, saying, "Quiet! Someone will hear you." Jacob continued, "It would be a good idea if we all returned quickly and with the least bit of fanfare to my house and go directly to my office. Also, before we leave, let's all help put the stones back where they were to cover the gap we just made in the wall."

Mark insisted on firmly holding the newly discovered misshapen gold ingot while the rest covered the gap in the wall with stones. As he held the gold, Mark felt his gold fever returning with its feeling of selfish possessiveness. He had felt it on previous treasure hunting expeditions. It could drive some men mad.

But he had learned to control it.

Upon their return to Jacob's office, they all had a smile on their faces. Everyone had a chance to hold the solid gold rock, feel the weight, and examine it. Then, Jacob placed it on top of his desk for them to gaze at in wonder. Jacob offered them champagne which they all accepted. Since most Israelis are also amateur archeologists, they all told stories about being on archeological digs for months where they found nothing or just some clay fragments of an ancient jar or pot.

Mark added, "It always feels so good to be on a successful treasure hunt." They all agreed and complimented his treasure hunting talent profusely.

Finally, Jacob said, "We all need to have a serious talk about how to manage this new discovery."

Mark was the first to speak, saying, "I think this rock weighs about three pounds. Therefore, if we calculate that gold is now selling for about two thousand dollars a troy ounce and there are 14.58 troy ounces to a pound multiplied by three, then this solid gold rock is worth more than eighty-seven thousand dollars and there are miles of it out there!"

The whole room stopped breathing for a moment when they realized the huge value of what they had just discovered! Luckily everyone in the room had the highest Israeli security clearance except Mark!

Jacob interjected, "What Mark just said scares me. Once this gets out, it will be impossible to control. Every amateur archeologist and treasure hunter will be out in force all over the country. They will dig up every wall in the country, including things that are built over them, such as highways or newer buildings, not to mention parts of the walls which are located in the West Bank!"

Shimon Weisman, the defense minister added, "What we need from Mark and Eric is an exact map of what walls and where they are located that have the hidden gold in them."

Mark replied, "I would be happy to prepare one with Eric's help."

Eric then mentioned, "I have thought of one more complication, which is that this gold was hidden by Temple priests for the Temple to use or rebuild. The Jewish faction that wants to see the Temple rebuilt could claim this gold to rebuild it." The meeting went silent at this comment.

Finally, the prime minister said, "This is the reason why the project must remain top secret. This project is too big for a team of archeologists to handle. So, I recommend we put the IDF on it as soon as we get the correct maps. That way we can hit it fast and hard before too many people find out exactly what's happening, and the general population gets wind of it."

The three members of the Mossad in the room shook their heads in disagreement.

In response, Alon Reuben, the director of Mossad, told the PM, "You are correct that this could get out of control very quickly, so I recommend a deception to keep control of it."

Sam added, "I think the soldiers engaged in this should wear uniforms and have signs saying Israel Electric Corporation." He continued, "The IEC is the largest supplier of electricity in Israel and the Palestinian territories and therefore a perfect cover to have men working on stone fences throughout Israel."

Everyone in the room thought this was an excellent idea. The PM looked at Sam and Eric and asked them to manage this project for the state. Both agreed immediately.

Before Sam left that night, he pulled Eric aside and personally congratulated him on his new rank of colonel but also told him, "Remember, based on my seniority of commission, I still outrank you."

Eric knew when he had to be full-tilt diplomatic, so as he saluted his friend Colonel Reichman, he said, "Yes, sir, of course! Sir!" Sam had a smile on his face as he returned Eric's salute.

Jacob added that it was getting late, and their wives must be getting worried, so he suggested they all continue to discuss this tomorrow. The party then ended. As Mark and Eric walked down the hill to their house, Mark turned to Eric and told him, "It's such an honor to be married to a colonel. But does that mean I will have to follow your orders?"

Eric replied, "Only when you do something bad."

To which Mark replied with a naughty gleam in his eyes, "I'm feeling bad tonight!"

Eric just shook his head and laughed. They both were laughing as they entered their home.

CHAPTER EIGHT

THE MANGER

The next two weeks were busy ones. The first problem was creating an accurate map of the stone walls filled with gold ingots. The stone walls went everywhere—south past Hebron to Be'er Shiva in the Negev; through the northern Galilee, and all through the Judean Hills and Samaria, including most of the West Bank. The second problem was organizing forty soldiers into squads tasked with as quietly and quickly as possible extracting the gold and bringing it to a central point for storage. It was determined that the best central point for the storage of the gold would be at three military bases: Ramat David, Hatzor and Hatzerim located across the country. The gold would be kept in locked rooms under guard at each place.

The retrieval of the gold based on the correct reading of the Copper Scroll treasure map went as well as could be expected since many of the stone blocks in the original walls had been lost or repurposed for other building projects. However, the one fact that made the hunting for these gold filled stone blocks easier was the team noticed that the Temple priests used a specific, dark cream colored limestone to manufacture these stone blocks. Therefore, it was easier to spot them compared to their surroundings, even when no longer in the walls but lying by the side of a new road, which cut through a wall or was repurposed for other construction projects. Mark and Eric both thought this slightly odd color had been picked on purpose by the ancient Temple priests to make it easier for the priests to identify the gold filled stone blocks.

As the prime minister had requested, Eric and Sam managed the project by forming teams to retrieve the gold. It was finally decided that because of the extreme confidentiality of the special assignment, the team, which totaled forty men plus Mark, Eric, and Sam, was only conscripted from the ranks of the Mossad and Sayeret Matkal. They all wore uniforms from the Israel Electric Corp (IEC) and did their work of breaking the stone blocks and removing the gold as unobtrusively and quickly as possible. Of course, the most important part of this treasure hunt was Mark and Eric's creation of the detailed map showing the walls where these gold filled ancient stones were located. The walls that still existed in open fields were the easiest from which to remove the gold except for the backbreaking work of moving and splitting the stone blocks under the hot sun. But as the walls approached new towns and villages, some of which were Arab, the work became dangerous as well.

Unfortunately, the walls closest to Jerusalem had been part of the destruction and rebuilding of the city so many times that it was economically impractical to dig through the modern city down so many layers to find the gold even when Mark's map showed exactly where the wall ran. The team had much better luck further away from Jerusalem, where there had been much less destruction and rebuilding and still many open spaces where the original wall was intact. Mark, Eric, and Sam were always out in the field supervising the various teams to make sure all the gold was accounted for, and everything went smoothly. Frequently, Eric participated in the very strenuous labor of extracting the gold from the limestone. Eric said that moving limestone blocks helped keep his muscles fit and also gave him a great tan. Sam and Mark just supervised. There were several times the team discovered that the stones had been reused for the new construction such as a farmer's wall, floor, or new border fence. But the Israeli or Arab farmer was always very happy to receive a new wall, floor, or fence to replace these old somewhat odd colored stone blocks. The team members just told the farmers they needed these particular stones because their color matched a building construction project on which they were working. Generally, the teams were in and out and done so quickly that collecting the gold went very smoothly except for one very dicey incident.

Toward the end of December during the holiday season, three young male Israeli teenagers were kidnapped by Islamic terrorists. It happened one afternoon while they were hitchhiking just outside of Jerusalem. The team members of the gold hunting expedition were quickly drafted into the hunt for these kids. The treasure hunt almost came to a dead stop. The entire country was looking for them.

However, while that country wide search was taking place, Eric and Sam, who were both retired from the military so therefore not officially included in the search effort, as well as Mark, continued to survey the stone walls for gold retrieval at a later date. Moreover, a few of these walls ran through some very remote places. Because of this and the fact the country was on alert for terrorists, Eric and Sam decided they should arm themselves while in the field. They decided to carry a semi-automatic Jericho 941 pistol, which was standard issue for both the IDF and the Israeli Special Forces. They also gave one to Mark to carry after a short course on how to use the pistol. The course basically boiled down to "keep the safety on at all times and your pistol in your holster unless you are actually going to shoot someone!"

Sam added with a smile, "Be careful you don't shoot your foot off or something even more valuable."

Both Sam and Eric laughed at this, but all Mark thought was that these Mossad guys had such a strange sense of humor sometimes. Mark had served in the US military as a second lieutenant and already knew his way around guns.

One such remote place was in the Judean Hills above the town of Bethlehem, which is located in the highly volatile West Bank. One day, during the late afternoon, they decided to survey the last section of stone wall before calling it quits for the day. The wall in which they were interested appeared to run up the side of a hill to the top and was mostly hidden by olive groves and palm trees. Although Sam was still built like a bull, he was getting a bit older, so he decided to stay down by the Jeep and let Eric and Mark hike up, following the wall to the top. Mark, as usual, wore his wide rim, brown Fedora hat given to him by his team when they had found King Herod's royal jewels on a previous treasure hunt.

Eric mentioned to Mark, "You look like a real adventurer and treasure hunter wearing that hat, boots, light brown khaki colored pants, shirt, and carrying a pistol—very dashing!" Mark smiled and blushed when he heard this from Eric. He didn't give Mark compliments very often.

When they both reached the top of the hill, they were surprised to see what looked like an ancient stone barn near the wall. It was completely hidden from the roads below and the surrounding countryside. Since they had previously discovered that repurposed, gold filled stone blocks had been used in other old buildings like this, their curiosity took over and they decided to explore it, even though it was now twilight. As they approached and entered, the archeologist in Eric immediately took over. The unlocked wooden door at the entrance easily swung open in spite of its age. They did not find any oddly colored stone blocks hiding Temple gold. However, Eric noted that the barn's rough-cut stone walls predated the wall that they were here to survey.

According to Eric, "The wooden ceiling beams are newer. They looked perhaps several hundred years old, but I am sure that these ancient stone barn walls are more than two thousand years old."

Mark also casually observed, "This looks like the perfect place to hide from the authorities. No one would ever find this hidden place." Additionally, they noticed the inside of the building looked like it was still a working barn. They both smelled the pungent odor of horse and sheep dung as well as drying hay. There also was a big opening cut like a window into the ancient rough stone wall on the backside of the farmhouse, which gave a clear view of the entire town of Bethlehem below. Additionally, there were animal stalls and six wooden animal feeding troughs and one stone one.

Eric explained, "These troughs that look like a baby's crib were also called a manger in ancient times. Indeed, just like the one in which Jesus was cradled after he was born when there was no room at the inn in Bethlehem, as the story goes."

But the item catching Mark's attention was the whip hanging in a furled circle on a rusty nail hammered into an old wooden post. As soon as Mark took down the whip, he gripped the handle tightly with his right hand and unfurled it. It felt so familiar to him. Mark explained to Eric, "This whip I am holding is a horse whip and is ten feet long and exactly the same as the one used by Indiana Jones in the movies. It is different from a bull whip, which is only eight feet long." Before Eric could ask how Mark knew this, Mark explained, "I spent three summers at a dude ranch in Texas as a teenager and was taught how to use a whip by a ranch hand called Old Jake. He was considered a master whip cracker. In addition to my other ranch chores and activities, I would practice on posts, fences, and trees for hours with him. I was fascinated with the cowboy culture as a teenager. During the third summer when Old Jake realized that I was a serious student of the art, he taught me some very advanced moves with a whip. But I confess that I have not touched a whip in decades but would enjoy showing you a few moves with the whip if you would like to see it." Mark sensed the minute he grabbed the handle of this horse whip his skill with it had come roaring back. Looking straight into Eric's surprised eyes, Mark simply said, "It all has to do with the flick of the wrist at the correct moment when the whip is in motion. It can be very cool to snap and crack the whip. Or, as Old Jake use to say to me, see how you can flick a fly off a horse's ass without bothering the horse."

Eric quickly asked Mark, "Please wait to demonstrate the whip. Since the cell phone reception around here is spotty at best, let me just run down the hill and get Sam. Sam would love to see you demonstrate a whip! Wait here! We'll be back in less than fifteen minutes." Mark yelled after him to hurry back since it was getting close to nightfall. With that, Eric turned and jogged down the hill, leaving Mark all alone in the ancient barn.

While alone, Mark decided to further explore the inside of the stone barn. The single stone manger aroused Mark's curiosity. Mark turned on his cell phone flashlight to get a better view since it was getting dark and there was no electricity or light in the old barn. The manger sat directly below the barn's only window. As far as Mark could tell, the window had never had any glass or wooden shutters, just a windowless opening cut into the stone wall. The trough or manger itself was full of debris and straw. On an impulse, Mark cleaned all the debris from it. Indeed, Mark saw it was like a crib, deep and big enough to hold a child.

But what completely surprised him was what he could now see on the clean stone surface at the bottom of the manger. Someone had carved the outline of a fish. Based on Mark's biblical studies, he knew instantly that the fish was the Greek symbol Christians used concurrently with the sign of the cross. The letters in the Greek word for fish spelled ICTHYS. However, the letters can also be the abbreviation for "Jesus Christ, Son of God, Savior." It was the symbol used by the earliest Christians to hide their faith from the Roman authorities. After this observation, he turned his cell phone light off, took the furled whip in his hand, and casually walked outside to the side of the barn with the view of the entire town of Bethlehem with its Church of the Nativity, the traditional site of the birth of Jesus. He wanted to contemplate the implications of what he had just found and enjoy the view below. He did not have a long time to think before he heard loud voices in Arabic and Hebrew coming from around the corner in the front yard of the barn.

Without revealing himself, Mark peered around the corner of the barn. What he saw shook him. There were three Israeli teenagers kneeling on the ground with their hands bound behind them. Standing very close to the kneeling teenagers were three adult men speaking Arabic, two of them wearing socks over their faces with cut-out slits for eyes, with one holding a very big knife, actually closer to a sword than a knife. The other hooded terrorist held a semi-automatic machine gun towards the teenagers. The third man, who wore no hood, was setting up a camera to film the scene. The men were all intensely focused on their efforts. Mark guessed these were the three kidnaped boys and more urgently, what was going to happen. These terrorists were going to behead these kids and film it. All Mark could think of was that he was going to let this happen over his dead body! He unconsciously started to unfurl his whip with his right hand and unholster and flip his pistol's safety off with his left. He had taught himself in the US army to be as good a shot with a pistol using either hand. As the whip unfurled, he felt a familiar surge of personal power when he heard the heavy leather cords of the whip hit the ground with a dull thud. What he had diplomatically not told Eric about his advanced whip training during that third summer was that Old Jake had also taught him how to kill or maim with a whip. This training came with one big caveat, to use it only under the most extreme circumstances, life or death. Mark knew this qualified. Getting hold of himself for a moment, Mark stopped to text Eric, luckily finding that this area had cell service, "Terrorists here! Help!" He then calmly put his cell phone in his pocket and stepped out from behind the corner of the barn while totally fixated on the would-be executioner. He noted he was about ten feet away, within whip range! Fortunately for Mark, they all had their backs to him, focusing on positioning the first teenager hostage for the best filming shots.

Very shortly, the terrorists started filming. As the one hooded man raised his hand holding his big knife to behead the first teenager, yelling, "Allahhu Akbar," all anyone could hear above the wind on that crisp December night was a soft whirl in the breeze and a very loud, snap-crackle sound cutting through the cool night air. The next instant the hooded, would-be executioner dropped his knife, which went spinning off into the surrounding dark bushes while both his hands were trying to desperately grasp the tightly wound leather bands of Mark's whip around his throat. The more he struggled to pull the leather bands free, the tighter they became. Before anyone could think what was happening or move, Mark yanked back on the whip with all his strength. This maneuver with the whip, tightened the leather bands into a death grip. The would-be executioner flew backwards, landing flat on his back as the leather bands of the whip around his throat slowly strangled him to death like a boa constrictor squeezing the life from its prey. As the terrorist gasped for breath, Mark knew that he alone was the only one who could release the whip's death grip.

The second hooded terrorist, seeing where the whip cord had come from, quickly turned to face Mark to fire his machine gun. But before he could fire, Eric jumped the terrorist from behind, putting him in a chokehold, causing him to drop the gun and lose consciousness. While this was happening, the third terrorist, who was behind the camera filming the execution of their hostages, turned and started to run. He ran directly into Sam which was like hitting a brick wall. Sam quickly put him in a headlock and searched him for weapons. After that, Sam appeared with the third terrorist walking beside him, bent over, immobilized in a headlock.

Immediately analyzing the scene, Sam told Mark, "Don't kill the terrorist choking on the ground. We need all of them to gather intelligence."

Acting on Sam's direction, Mark flicked his wrist, which caused the leather cord of the whip to ripple to its end, making it unwind and fall quickly and harmlessly away from the terrorist's throat, thereby allowing him to breathe and saving his life. However, they could all see the fight had completely drained from him while he lay on the ground violently coughing and gasping for air. Mark proceeded to rewind his whip and put his pistol away. Glad he did not have to use it.

Sam could not help himself when he yelled to Mark, "Remember to put your safety back on!"

Actually, in the excitement, Mark had forgotten to do it. So, he yelled back, "Thank you, Sam."

In the meantime, Eric had found a spot where his cell phone worked and was calling the IDF and Shin Bet, Israel's security service, telling them what had occurred and where. Mark quickly walked over to the three teenagers and untied the ropes that bound their hands behind them. They were beyond happy that they were alive and free and had witnessed everything. They were so ecstatic that they showered Mark with hugs and compliments, and one even kissed him on the cheek. Mark kept an eye on Eric during this display of admiration. He thought he even saw a flicker of jealousy or at least surprise at this behavior on Eric's face. Mark thought the evening could not get any better when he noticed this. He thought it balanced the relationship. Because of Eric's movie star good looks and hero exploits, it was Eric who usually was the object of such attention.

It took less than fifteen minutes for the IDF and the Shin Bet to arrive. Afterwards, the place was crawling with soldiers and police. By then it was getting close to midnight as the stars and full moon lit up the night sky. The moonlight was so strong over the Judean Hills that it clearly reflected its shimmering beauty at night.

A couple of hours later, when everyone was leaving, Mark asked Sam, "Would you mind if you hitched a ride back home with the IDF? I want to be alone up here with Eric for a while. We will drive back home in Eric's Land Rover when we're ready."

Sam had no problem with that and departed, saying, "I'll see you both tomorrow to continue the wall project."

Eric was a little surprised that Mark wanted to stay on top of this secluded hill, but sensed Mark needed to discuss something.

As soon as everyone had departed, Mark turned towards Eric, saying, "I have discovered something in the barn that I want you to see." When they entered the barn, Mark proceeded to turn on his cell phone light to show Eric the carved fish on the bottom of the stone trough.

Eric's eyes widened when he saw it, realizing the full implication of the carving. He immediately asked, *Could this be the real manger where Jesus was born, up here in this secret place?*

However, before Eric could say anything, Mark asked him, "Just to clarify where we are. Who owns this barn and land around it?"

Eric replied, "The Catholic Church owns it, going back for as long as there are property records."

Mark then asked, "In what township is this land located?"

Eric answered, "The wall with the gold filled blocks that we are surveying, and we know is approximately two thousand years old, dating to the time of the Temple and Jesus, is also the border between the town of Bethlehem and private land ownership on the other side. So, this stone barn and manger are definitely located in the town of Bethlehem." These answers seemed to verify their new discovery. Eric added, "I want to check one more thing." He put his own cell phone flashlight up close to the fish carving and bent down close to it himself so he could see better. He then explained to Mark, "The engravings in rock or limestone over the centuries develop a certain coating at the bottom of the carving's etches. The coating can be scrapped off to verify the exact age. Recent fakes do not have it. It is one way scientists can distinguish if a relic is authentic." He then bent down again to take a closer look with his trained archeologist's eyes at the fish carving, and sure enough, he saw it had developed the centuries old or possibly much older coating at the bottom of the carving's etches. Eric turned to Mark, took a breath, and said, "I am astounded at your luck or unerring instinct to find treasure, or in this case, religious treasure."

All Mark softly said in response so as to ignore the compliment and change the subject was to ask Eric if he remembered that this was Christmas Eve, and it was almost midnight. Eric replied that he had forgotten. So, they both decided to walk outside to relax and listen to the choirs and the festivities of Bethlehem spread below them. They sat on a rock on the edge of the top of the hill to contemplate what they had just found and watch Bethlehem lit up with the lights of many Christmas trees and multicolored streetlights. They held each other close for warmth as they also heard the choirs singing God's praises and the songs of thousands of pilgrims singing and praying to God. They both could deeply feel the faith in God below them. The sounds echoed straight up the hill and into the stone barn through the windowless opening in the stone wall behind which lay the manger. Mark instantly realized that the hill acted as a kind of church and the ancient stone barn its nave. He realized that the prayers of all the pilgrims in the town below were funneled to heaven from here. When both Eric and Mark came to know this, a serenity settled over them.

Suddenly, they heard something behind them. It was three Christian monks slowly walking along an unseen ancient path to the barn with their heads hooded and bowed and hands clasped in prayer. They ignored Eric and Mark's presence.

When they arrived before the open window of the ancient barn, they knelt and prayed. Their heads bowed before the window and stone manger behind it. Just then, as it turned midnight, all the big bells of the many Christian churches below began to ring—sending their sounds echoing up the hill and into the barn. Adding moonlight streaming into the ancient barn, bathing the stone manger with the starry sky above it, the scene became powerfully spiritual, even magical.

In spite of Mark and Eric being secular Jews, they felt the scene unfolding before them was breathtaking in its spiritual simplicity. After a while, they both agreed it was time for them to leave the monks to their prayers in this magical place. As they slowly walked down to Eric's Jeep and drove home, they also agreed not to tell anyone what they had discovered for fear of creating controversy over the true birthplace of Jesus and changing this peaceful and spiritual place with thousands of pilgrims. Just before they both fell asleep in each other's arms that night, at peace with the world, Eric whispered to Mark, "You're my hero."

CHAPTER NINE

THE HONEYPOT

Dictionary definition of a honeypot: a jar or earthen pot containing sweet honey made from bee's nectar.

The intelligence community or espionage definition of a honeypot: a trap or covert operation designed to attract, capture, or assassinate enemies or spies using romantic or sexual enticements. The idea is to create an appealing target that entices individuals to reveal their true intentions or engage in activities that could be monitored or controlled. It is mostly used under heterosexual circumstances. BUT NOT ALWAYS! The concept is simple but dangerously effective.

The gold retrieval project took about eight weeks of intense work to complete, finishing in midwinter. At the end of the project, Mark, Eric, and Sam calculated that they were able to retrieve about 50 percent of the gold hidden in the limestone blocks by the Temple priests, which totaled about three hundred million dollars.

The prime minister and the entire military high command of Israel were extremely pleased with the final result of this secret project. The only other person made aware of the treasure hunt was the Israeli minister of finance. He had to be informed since there was an additional three hundred million dollars' worth of gold hitting the treasury and that amount in gold had to be explained. At the end of the treasure hunt, the government gave a party at Mossad headquarters for the entire team to thank everyone for their efforts. At Jacob's recommendation, Mark and Eric negotiated (actually insisted), with the prime minister to give all team members an equivalent to a six month salary bonus as a special "thank you" for all their hard work. The prime minister made the announcement of the bonus at the party in hope of scoring some political points with the crowd. But the entire team knew it was Mark and Eric's fine handiwork in arranging it.

Also, at the party, the Israeli minister of finance introduced himself to Mark and immediately gave Mark a big bear hug and kiss on the cheek. Then he announced to all there, "Because of this and past successful treasure hunts that Mark originated, Israel's currency, the shekel, has so much gold backing it that it is now one of the strongest currencies in the world, equivalent to the Swiss franc. So, I want to thank Mark and Eric too for their contribution to this."

Pointing to Eric, Mark responded to his praise and kiss by saying, "Thank you, but you better be careful not to make him jealous."

Eric just smiled a half smile while he slightly shook his head in mild disagreement and resignation at another of Mark's spur of the moment comments. Afterwards, Mark, out of the corner of his eye, continued to notice with pride in his husband that Eric was turning heads more than ever with his new dark tan from his recent manual labor moving stone blocks in the fields.

At the end of the party as people were leaving, both Alon Reuben, the director and Gideon Avraham, the assistant director of the Mossad, approached Eric to say goodnight but also asked him if he wouldn't mind meeting with them at the Mossad headquarters tomorrow at 11:00 a.m. in Alon's office. Eric agreed but was on guard about the meeting since he knew these two were very busy men and did not schedule meetings simply to pass the time. Something told him not to tell Mark about the meeting.

The meeting started promptly at 11:00 a.m. with the newly promoted Colonel Eric Jansen, retired, sitting in the director's office with both the director and assistant director also present.

Alon Reuben started the meeting by saying he wanted to get straight to the point. He continued, "There is an assignment that we both feel you are perfect for. It involves an older, Egyptian senior diplomat based at the Egyptian embassy in Paris who has two hobbies —very handsome men and archeology. He also has access to certain vital information Israel needs. It is a deluxe assignment all the way. You would have a substantial expense account to accomplish it."

Gideon Avraham interjected, "Because of your looks, excellent language skills, proficiency in sports, your world famous reputation as an archeologist, and lastly, your very large endowment, you would be perfect for the job."

Eric's reaction was instantaneously negative. So much so, that he stood up, turned, and began to leave.

Just before he opened the door to leave, Gideon Avraham, added, "This assignment would also ultimately involve the assassination of the target and possibly a bodyguard or two."

Eric stopped, turned, and loudly said to both men, "So it doesn't matter to you that I'm retired and happily married, but you still want me to fuck this guy, kill him and betray my own marriage with every touch at the same time? You are both a piece of work. Never call me again!" With that Eric left, slamming the door behind him.

When Eric was gone, both Alon and Gideon looked at each other. Then Alon calmly said, "I told you it was too soon to push him. He needs a vacation. I shouldn't have listened to you. And I still think he is our best operative. Also, you shouldn't be so jealous just because he has become so politically popular." Gideon said nothing in response to his boss—just sat there. They also both knew Eric was a natural born hunter/killer and excellent at the job. They counted on Eric's impulse to kill without penalty or retribution to bring him around. And if this assignment was not timed correctly for Eric, there would be other assignments for him in the future. However, what they didn't foresee was the stabilizing influence of Eric's relationship with Mark.

On the way back, driving to his house, Eric's brain started analyzing what had just happened. He particularly focused on their use of the phrase "large endowment." He asked himself, *How does the Mossad know about that?* He came to the conclusion there were only two ways the Mossad could have learned about it. From his car he called Mark, who was busy reading an archeological journal before starting to make lunch. He told Mark, "Instead of making lunch, I will pick you up at home in fifteen minutes and drive to a small outdoor cafe we both know in Haifa."

Even before Mark sat in Eric's Land Rover, he knew something was wrong by Eric's tone on the phone. However, Eric didn't say a word the entire trip and motioned to Mark not to speak either. The cafe was almost deserted, which is why

Eric chose it. They ordered lunch as soon as they were seated. After that, Eric asked Mark, "Have you noticed anything odd around the house lately?"

Mark immediately answered, "No."

Eric then asked Mark, "Please explain your off-hand comment that you made at Jacob's party about using the front door this time which everyone thought was funny."

Mark, sensing this was important, explained, "The morning that you left to go catch terrorists, I awoke to an empty house and was a bit frantic with worry. So, I ran up to Jacob's house to ask him his advice and if he knew anything about where you went. I had a bit of trouble getting in and was drugged by some ice tea Noah served me with Jacob's approval. The other people at Jacob's house were Major General Chiam Savage, Shimon Weisman, Minister of Defense and Gideon Avraham, who made a nasty crack about gay people. Sam's wife, Alisa Reichman, was also there later. She set me straight that the government was already helping you and they didn't want me to fly to Cairo to mess things up. I hope you are not angry with me for not telling you, but I was embarrassed by the incident and Jacob said you were back home so quickly anyway."

It took Eric a minute to process this story he had not heard before. He decided to reveal some things to Mark and replied,

"First, I am not in any way angry or upset with you for trying to ride to my rescue! Second, I just attended a meeting at Mossad headquarters, which I did not tell you about. Sorry! They wanted me to act as a honeypot to some old man to get important intelligence from him. What they didn't say, but I know, is that sometimes these covert honeypot operations can take years to develop, and that with every touch, I would be betraying our marriage and you. Third, Sam's wife, Alisa, who I like very much, is also an active, not retired, Mossad agent. Fourth, I want you to fire Noah immediately. He can no longer have access to our home because I suspect our house is bugged and he may be the culprit. It's possible our cars are too. That is the reason we are having lunch at this outside cafe. And lastly, we are going back home after lunch and go through the house searching for hidden webcams and listening bugs. I have the device that can detect all of them in the garage. Our etiquette inside our house until I finish de-bugging it is that we do not speak to each other until it's finished. You can just sit and read. I will do it all. For the record, unbeknown to you, I did this shortly after we moved in, but I am now sure it has since been compromised." Eric stopped short of telling Mark that their neighbor and good friend, Jacob Kurtz, was the head of a super-secret agency to which all Israeli intelligence agencies reported. An agency which had given the order to assassinate dozens of Israel's enemies. In other words, underneath Jacob's extremely sophisticated and charming exterior, there was a killer who was the most politically powerful man in Israel.

Eric thought, *It takes a killer to know a killer.* So, he just added, "I know he is our friend. But be careful what you say to Jacob in the future."

Mark was nonplussed when he heard all this but recovered quickly. He calmly asked Eric, "What alerted you to this all of a sudden?"

Eric replied, "During the assignment interview, the assistant director of Mossad, Gideon Avraham, said one of the reasons that I was perfect for the assignment was my very large endowment. There was only two ways he could have found out about that. First, if you were bragging to someone. Or the second is, if the Mossad had the house bugged."

Mark seriously responded, "I have never said anything like that to anyone other than to you and then only as a compliment when we make love."

All Eric said in response was that he had already guessed this, adding, "Let's go back to the house now and yank out all those bugs!"

Before they left, Mark asked Eric to consider a theory. "I think the prime minister considers you a political threat. I think that it is not out of the bounds of possibility that the PM instigated this honeypot assignment through the Mossad to veer you offtrack and eliminate you as a political rival."

Eric stopped in his tracks, took a short minute to consider this, and said to Mark, "My partner is so smart. It's a little conspiratorial. But not far fetched. I will discover the truth of it." Eric thought for another second, then told Mark, "You could be right. Gideon Avraham is used by the prime minister as his attack dog."

Back at their house, as agreed, Mark took a seat on the living room couch and read. Eric retrieved his multi-frequency bug detector from the garage and put on his cell phone flashlight while he systematically searched every nook and corner of the house. As he explained to Mark later, "Mini video spy cams give off a radio frequency which can be detected by my handheld radio frequency detector. Additionally, many mini audio surveillance devices give off a small red or green light or reflect when a flashlight is shined on them in a dark space. Since both types of these spy devices need direct lines of sight or unobstructed listening space and also unimpeded electricity to power them, they are not that hard to find once you are aware of their presence and where to look. They are usually near or inside a source of electricity such as an electrical outlet, light switch, ceiling fan, smoke detector, lamp, lightbulb, or behind a grate." Less than two hours later, Eric had found and dismantled fourteen such devices throughout the house and pool area including in each of their four bedrooms. Lastly, Eric asked Mark for the keys to Mark's car, saying, "I am now going to debug our two cars as well."

Mark was shocked when he saw Eric with more than fourteen devices dangling from his hand. First thing Eric said to Mark was, "I'm sure I got them all. So, now call our chef, Noah, and fire him."

Mark did this immediately. Next Eric changed the biometric security codes on the front and pool doors, cancelling Noah's access. After all this, they both seemed to relax a little. Mark poured them both a glass of excellent Israeli red wine as they sank into their couch in the living room and cuddled close together. It was clear to both of them that they were still unnerved by this invasion of privacy. They sat on the couch for almost an hour drinking wine without speaking.

Finally, Mark turned to Eric and said, "Because we yanked out all the eavesdropping devices, the Mossad or whoever has been listening and videotaping us will now know we are aware of what they did."

Eric replied, "Exactly. This dots the eye on my refusal to accept their honeypot assignment."

Mark responded, "Let's be realistic, those sex videos of you and me are still out there, and if I am correct and the PM was behind your honeypot assignment to derail your political career, then the videos probably will be made public during your campaign for office." Mark added with a sly smile, "Of course, there are some neighborhoods in Tel Aviv that would elect you king if they saw those videos!"

They both burst out laughing at this. Trying to ignore Mark's sense of humor, Eric thought for a moment before he spoke. "About my political career, I was meaning to tell you that I decided to put it on hold. There is an ancient Roman galleon that sunk off the coast of Sicily. My contacts tell me that their initial exploration shows that it was likely loaded with treasure from Rome's war with Persia when it sank. In other words, I think it has a strong possibility of being a treasure galleon. I was wondering if we might put together an archeological expedition to go look/see what we can find."

Mark immediately said, "I think that's a great idea. We need another adventure."

Eric continued that he needed to tell Mark something else, "I wouldn't have had the strength to turn down that honeypot assignment without your love and strength."

Now it was Mark's turn to think for a moment. Then he said, "I need to tell you something I never told you before. Even though it's been almost four years, every time we make love, it's like the first time for me."

With this confession, Eric embraced Mark and said it was the same for him. But Eric then added, "Before we continue, I have another secret to tell you."

Mark braced himself for the worst, thinking, *It's been a day of secrets—what brick is going to drop on me now?*

Eric nonchalantly said, "I can cook. In fact, I have been told that I am a good cook when I need to be. However, I know you love cooking so I never interfered, but we just fired our part time chef, so I think it's time you knew this."

All of a sudden there was a big smile on Mark's face when he responded, "You mean I married a cook! My day just got much better!" So, Mark half joked, "We can compare recipes!"

Eric's reaction was immediate as he winced in feigned pain.

However, Mark ignored Eric's response and continued, "I guess there's still more to you than meets the naked eye!" They proceeded to make love on their couch, unobserved, in the privacy of their own home. It felt like their first time.

CHAPTER TEN

·⌒ঙ৶ঙ⌒·

THE TENERIFE KILL ZONE

Early the next morning Eric's military psychologist, Lieutenant Colonel Rachel Stein called, wanting to set up a therapy session with both Eric and Mark. She didn't like that they had been ignoring her. And she reminded Eric that he needed to be officially cleared by the military, meaning her. It was true. They had been ignoring Eric's therapy sessions for his PTSD since Eric had returned from Africa and had killed the terrorist, Mohammed Al Kaduna, thinking or hoping that Eric had been cured. However, they both thought it was best politically to see Rachel officially one more time for closure. So, they arranged to see her that day.

On the way, driving to the therapy session, Mark asked Eric if he thought that Rachel's call was prompted by them stripping their home of the Mossad webcams and listening spy devices.

Eric answered, "I don't know, but remember in Israel everything is connected to everything. So keep your eyes and ears open."

When they arrived at Rachel's office, she went out of her way to make them feel comfortable, offering them coffee or tea and biscuits, even complimenting them that they were the most famous couple she had ever treated. When they were all seated, she stated, "In order for me to recommend to the military that Eric's case be closed, you both will have to do one last thing. And that is, the government wants you both to spend two weeks on a vacation paid for by the government at a five star holistic wellness spa and hotel just outside the capital of Santa Cruz de Tenerife in the Spanish Canary Islands off the coast of Africa. It is owned by an Israeli who is also former Mossad. And I have sent many Israeli soldiers there over the years, and they all said it helped them recover from their emotional problems, including PTSD. The holistic treatments at the spa include yoga, massages, facials, acupuncture, meditation, group sessions, and healthy meals by famous chefs. All treatments are optional. And there are therapists on staff if needed." Mark immediately loved the idea.

All Eric said was, "I have heard of this place for traumatized soldiers to recuperate. The feedback I've received has been positive. It is supposed to be quite beautiful, and the weather is warm enough to swim in the winter. But most importantly, the fact that it is owned and managed by a former Mossad operative serving Israeli soldiers as well as the general public is not widely known or advertised so it makes the resort very secure."

Knowing Eric's psychological make-up so well, Rachel mentioned to him, "I also heard that you could hike or climb up to the rim of a huge and sometimes active volcano on the island if you wanted." This sealed the deal for Eric as she knew it would.

He said, "I have never hiked to the rim of a volcano and I am definitely looking forward to doing it."

Two last requests that Dr. Stein made were, "Please refrain from telling anyone where you are going on vacation, and take it relatively soon."

Mark was so excited about visiting the Canary Islands that he failed to catch the full significance of her requests. He simply thought that she was protecting Eric's reputation. Eric agreed to her requests while saying nothing more. Driving back home, they agreed that it would be fun to go to this spa and they could still plan a trip to dive off the coast of Sicily to find ancient Roman treasure in a sunken galleon afterwards in the summer.

Upon returning home Eric spent time researching the volcano on Tenerife and found that it is called the Tiede Volcano located in the middle of Tiede National Park and is the highest peak in Spain at 12,198 feet. He also discovered that there is a cable car that can take tourists to 8,000 feet with the final 4,198 feet done by hiking in good weather the rest of the way or by mountain climbing up the almost sheer north face to the rim of the volcano's crater. Adding to Eric's challenge was that during the wintertime, when they were planning to visit, the top to the volcano was encased in snow and ice, even though it's warm enough to swim below at sea level.

When Eric realized the height of the volcano's rim, he knew he had to begin his high altitude training immediately. So, after finishing his research, he proceeded to his extreme fitness gym where they had a facility for high altitude training. He needed to begin that same day preparing for the high attitude ascent because it takes weeks to properly acclimate. It would consist of him running on a special treadmill each day, gradually increasing the time. This treadmill was enclosed in a special airtight glass box where every day there would be less and less oxygen pumped in, which gradually simulates higher and higher altitudes with less biometric pressure and oxygen. Eric, being an expert mountain climber, knew this type of high altitude training would prevent high altitude sickness. He also increased his extreme workout routine to include rock wall climbing two stories up; switching to a two hundred foot rope stretched above the gym that he traversed with hand over hand motion to the other side before rappelling down by rope. All done without a safety net. While he was in training, Eric knew Mark well enough to know that the volcano rim was too high an altitude for Mark to attempt—even the cable car ride was too high for him. So, he thought Mark would adjourn to the much lower mountain lodge to enjoy the view if he visited the volcano at all. He also planned on bringing all his own mountain climbing gear with him which he would send ahead. On an accent like this, Eric knew that his mountain climbing equipment was critically important. It could make the difference between life and death, and he was not going to rely on any rented equipment. He also knew he would not be allowed to attempt it alone. So, he was also looking forward to meeting his expert mountain climbing teammates that the government insisted on choosing for his own safety. In spite of anything, he was going to be ready for the accent to the rim!

Just for fun, several weeks later, before they left for the Canary Islands, Mark and Eric decided to give a Valentine's Day party in their home for personal friends. However, it did not turn out that way. Everyone who was any one in Israel came. They couldn't prevent it and it would become political when the newspapers reviewed it the next day. The newspapers asked, "Is Eric Jansen running for political office? Is he the next prime minister?" Eric really didn't care what the newspapers said since he had decided to delay his entrance into politics. Nevertheless, two major surprises at their party occurred. The first was when Jacob Kurtz arrived with Miriam Jansen, Eric's mother, as his date. They told Mark, Eric, and Eric's brother, David and Susan, his wife, who were all together at the party at the same time that they had been dating since meeting on the plane when they all flew to New York City and were soon planning to announce their engagement. They were going to have a big engagement party in about a month to announce it formally but wanted the family to know first. They then left to find Jacob's family— Ariel Kurtz, his son, and his wife, Julie. Mark looked at Eric after Jacob and his mother had gone. Even though he and all of the family had congratulated them on their engagement, Mark could tell it had really surprised Eric and it was taking a while for him to process it. Eric was happy for his mother, but something was bothering him about it that Mark could not understand. Mark thought it was probably Eric's mother/son relationship being shaken a bit. But Mark discovered much later, it was really Jacob's license-to-kill alternate life which troubled him for his mother's sake.

The second surprise at their Valentine's Day party was something much more unnerving to Mark. Jethro, the invaluable young military pilot who had assisted them on their previous treasure hunting expedition to Mount Karkom in the Negev desert, pulled Mark aside at the party for a private discussion. During the last few years, Jethro had resigned from the military and opened a successful construction business located in the towns in the Negev. Mark considered Jethro a trusted friend, who was still connected with the military and political events in Israel, especially in the Negev, sort of a quasi-desert chieftain. Jethro got straight to the point when they were alone. He alerted Mark when he said, "Due to your high profile gay marriage and notoriety as successful treasure hunters who have enhanced the economy and stature of Israel with the discovery of huge amounts of treasure, but more importantly, Eric's reputation for killing important Islamic terrorists, you and Eric have become number one on the revenge list of major Islamic terrorist groups around the world. I have also heard that you both have incurred the extreme jealousy of some current senior government politicians due to Eric's political popularity. I just want to make sure that you both are aware of this and be on guard, especially when or if you travel abroad from Israel."

Mark was stunned when he heard this. He realized immediately that Jethro had spoken the truth and could not believe he had not thought of the danger himself. Mark thanked Jethro for his warning. As they returned to the party,

Mark thought himself so stupid for not realizing earlier that, *The assassin's knife cuts both ways!* He considered himself forewarned. That night, he mentioned the warning of possible assassination to Eric, who just said he was always aware of the possibility, but Mark should relax and enjoy their upcoming vacation. Eric had put on his most noncommittal face in response so Mark could not tell whether he was really worried or not. Actually, no one can read a Mossad "poker face." It was one of their trademarks.

The only other interesting thing that Mark observed at their Valentine's Day party occurred when Mark saw Eric and Jacob engaged in a deep private conversation towards the end of the party just before Jacob and Miriam left. Mark dismissed this observation as unimportant.

Mark and Eric departed for the Canary Islands a week later from Ben Gurion Airport in Tel Aviv. Only a few people knew where they were going. Eric had sent all his mountain climbing gear ahead so it would be waiting for him at the hotel upon arrival. Their flights on Iberia Airways went from Tel Aviv to Madrid, then a change of planes to Tenerife, the largest island in the Canary Islands located in the Atlantic Ocean off the coast of Africa.

While traveling on the plane, Mark turned to Eric and said, "I bet it's not like flying at supersonic speed on *Dragon Fire?*"

Eric smiled as he answered, "Actually, it's a lot more comfortable and we're in no rush. It will get us there." The only two somewhat pleasant surprises on their low-key trip to Tenerife occurred when Eric was recognized at Tel Aviv's Ben Gurion Airport and the whole crowd started to applaud. He just gave them his victory sign with his two fingers and then tried to ignore the stares. The next pleasant surprise came while they were waiting to change planes in Madrid, when two teenage Israeli girls approached Eric to ask him for his autograph. Of course, he gave it to them. However, Mark and Eric were both still chuckling about it as they boarded the aircraft to Tenerife.

During the flight, Eric shared with Mark that an old friend, Dimitri Sokolov, from his days with the Israeli Special Forces, had just confirmed before they boarded that he would be joining Eric on his mountain climbing expedition to the rim of the volcano. Eric explained that Dimitri was an avid mountaineer like himself and for safety sake, all climbers should not climb alone. In fact, he continued, Dimitri was more experienced at climbing mountains than Eric and he felt lucky to be climbing with him. So, Eric thought this should put Mark's mind at ease about the climb. Also, he was looking forward to seeing his old friend again and hoped Mark would like Dimitri too.

As the plane approached Santa Cruz, the largest town on Tenerife, the volcano or Tiede Peak as the locals call it, dominated everything. From the plane it looked like it covered about half the island.

To Mark it looked prehistoric with its sandy colored bare rock face alternating between sheer slopes ending in giant jagged fissures with its top covered in snow looming over the island. Mark thought, *It's so tall even birds don't fly that high.* In fact, from his broad view from the plane as they landed, it looked to him like a deathtrap for all mountain climbers. But he said nothing to Eric.

Eric, on the other hand, when he first saw the volcano, got a rush of adrenaline through his veins that only a true mountain climber can explain. It appeared to him as a great challenge. He had been high altitude training for this accent six-to-eight hours every day since they agreed to go. He was ready. He was in the best shape he had ever been. He told Mark that he had done his homework on the volcano, and he had discovered it was still active. So, he had brought an oxygen mask with him not only for the extreme height but for any poisonous sulfur fumes at the top. He was also thrilled that he would be able to look into the crater from its rim to see the rivers of molten lava. He was so excited he could hardly contain himself. Unconvinced of the climb's safety and concern for Eric, Mark became very quiet for the rest of the trip. He realized this mountain climbing ascent was going to be much more dangerous than he had foreseen, and he could not stop Eric from going. Their landing was on time and uneventful. The hotel, however, was a delightful surprise, starting with the hotel's representative, who greeted them at the airport. His name was Ari Segal. He was their driver, their guide, and also the leader of their optional group therapy sessions.

He greeted them with a warm smile while saying, "Welcome to the Canary Islands and Tenerife. I will be your driver and guide during your stay at The Secret Hideaway Hotel."

Mark and Eric discovered that Ari was Israeli, but the rest of the hotel staff came from all over Europe. The hotel itself was located on the beach almost at the tip of the island which made it a bit isolated. But because it was also the last one on the hotel strip, the hotel was able to construct small, detached villas climbing up the side of a contiguous volcanic lava hill. The villas were all built in the Greek Mediterranean style, with whitewashed domed roofs and white exteriors covered in lush purple and dark red bougainvillea flowers, clay potted red geraniums on the many terraces and sweet smelling lavender in shades of violet planted everywhere. What made this first impression very dramatic was the utter desolation of the surrounding dark volcanic lava rock just beyond the planted areas.

The Israeli government had reserved for them one of these charming villas located a short walk from the main hotel. Mark was very impressed with the interior design of this exclusive hotel, which combined Greek mediterranean exteriors with African interior design, a nod to how close they were to Africa. The combination was striking and very luxurious. Eric duly noted that his big box full of mountaineering gear was waiting for him in their villa.

But before unpacking, Eric searched the villa for any listening bugs or webcams. He found three. Holding them in his hand, he said to Mark, "Not unexpected since the place is actually owned and managed by the Mossad."

Mark simply replied, "The Mossad also knew you would find them." This comment brought a big smile to Eric's face.

After quickly unpacking everything but Eric's box full of gear, they decided to stroll around the hotel to check it out. They discovered Ari waiting in the hotel lobby to show them around. Apparently, Eric's fame had preceded them when the entire hotel staff already knew all about him and his exploits. Both of them became increasingly aware on this trip that Eric had become a famous Israeli national hero.

Ari started the tour by showing them the hotel's huge round saltwater pool situated at the ocean's edge so that the spray from the waves, indeed, entire waves would overflow into the pool. A row of low-rise chunks of lava rock separated the pool's edge from the ocean, creating a wonderful spray when the ocean waves hit the rocks. Mark and Eric couldn't wait to go swimming in it. Ari also told them, "This time of the year the weather is perfect for outside yoga classes by the pool where you can feel the gentle warm African breezes coming ashore. The yoga and meditation classes are part of the hotel's holistic therapy program. And there is a covered area at the end of a lava rock trail overlooking the pool and ocean with a hammock in which you can just do nothing while relaxing and swinging in the hammock."

Inside the hotel, Ari proudly showed them the restaurants. He said, "The first one is rated four stars and is considered one of the best in all the islands. It also serves full room service to all the rooms, including the villas. The second restaurant is a kosher restaurant, the only one in the Canary Islands and is always busy."

But what caught Mark's eye was the bar in the first restaurant. The entire base of the bar was a glass enclosed aquarium lit so not only could you see the side of the aquarium facing the restaurant, but when you were sitting at it and looked down, you could also see all the tropical fish swimming under the glass top of the aquarium bar. The bar also had a narrow black leather pad running along the corner edge where you could put your elbows while drinking. Mark was enthralled with the idea. And Eric was glad that Mark was enjoying himself.

Additionally, Ari mentioned, "Watching the fish in the aquarium can be very therapeutic."

Lastly, Ari showed them the spa area with a well equipped gym area next to it. The spa was a true Turkish hammam or Turkish bath. It had a wet steam room, a dry steam room, a cold water plunge pool and a huge rectangular block of creamy white alabaster more than big enough for two people to get massaged at the same time, set in the center of a domed room with walls covered in white marble and second story windows letting in natural sunlight.

This was it for Mark. He turned to Eric and told him, "Tomorrow's schedule is room service for breakfast. Then we go swimming in the pool with lunch poolside. Then massage for two with the full hammam spa treatment. Then drinks and dinner. Let's book the massage now."

Eric knew when to just nod his head in agreement. Besides he was beginning to enjoy this posh hotel himself. That night they ate at the four star rated hotel restaurant. The Spanish tapas on the menu were so good and so many that they ate nothing else but also managed to consume two bottles of excellent red Spanish wine. They went to sleep a little drunk and a little tired but very relaxed.

The next day they followed the schedule Mark had planned. Breakfast in the room was on time and excellent, followed by making love, then a swim in the saltwater pool, a light lunch poolside and a Turkish bath in the afternoon. They followed the full Turkish bath regimen. The full Turkish bath was not only a means to get clean. It is a ritualistic experience with hot steam, detoxifying body treatments with plenty of water or iced tea to drink. This hydrotherapy treatment was supposed to have a miraculous effect on both your physical and mental state. The hot steam had a relaxing effect on their bodies, promoting sweating and the elimination of toxins. It consisted of about fifteen minutes in a hot wet steam room, next ten minutes in a dry steam room, but then a thirty-second dip into a very cold water plunge pool to close the pores and tone their bodies. After that, wrapped in a towel around the waist, Eric and Mark lay down on the flat stone slab for a massage, which consisted of perfumed oils smelling like a mixture of eucalyptus and lavender. Each had their own exceptionally beautiful female masseuse who rubbed oil all over their bodies, then proceeded to exfoliate their skin with a rough sponge, followed by a very deep tissue, even at times painful, body massage. All this happened under about two feet of soapy bubbles. The only part of their bodies not covered in deep bubbles were their heads. When they turned over and were facing up, something happened that surprised and deeply effected Mark. Eric reached over and gently held Mark's hand as they lay side by side, hidden under a mountain of bubbles, with the two beautiful female masseuses feverishly working on their bodies. Mark thought it was such a surprising yet intimate, gentle, loving secret gesture, hidden under all those bubbles! After the massages, they went into the town of Santa Cruz for a short stroll around the port. They were both amazed at how clean and pretty the town and harbor were. It looked like a Mediterranean village by the ocean. They also both noticed that there were many gay couples walking and holding hands together. Both of them knew that Gran Canaria Island was the center of gay life in the Canary Islands but they were surprised to see gay life so prevalent and accepted in Santa Cruz too. Mark guessed that Santa Cruz was more for gay couples and Gran Canaria was more for gay singles. In any case, they both felt relaxed enough to hold hands in public for the first time in their relationship as they walked.

This heavenly and relaxed mood dramatically changed at dinner. They both were in the hotel's restaurant sitting at the aquarium bar. They had just ordered their first glass of wine while looking down, trying to count the many types of tropical fish, when from behind came a booming voice, "Hello, pretty boy!"

With that, the stranger proceeded to give Eric a big wet kiss on his cheek, just missing his mouth, while giving him a big bear hug and grabbing Eric's crotch. Still grabbing Eric's crotch, he turned to Mark and said, "You want to share his very large endowment? Do you and pretty boy do threesomes?"

Mark was nonplussed, speechless.

But even more surprising was Eric's reaction. Instead of pushing the stranger away and knocking him out cold, Eric had a big smile on his face and returned the man's hug, saying, "I have been waiting for you." With that, he introduced Dimitri Sokolov, his old friend and fellow former member of the Israeli Special Forces.

Dimitri was about Eric's age. He had dark red hair and green eyes and a short black beard, like he had missed shaving for two days.

Mark immediately saw that Dimitri was also in excellent physical shape like Eric. In a nutshell, Mark thought Dimitri was extremely handsome and ruggedly sexy. He also knew competition when he saw it!

Eric went on to explain to Mark, "Dimitri is the old friend that I told you about."

Regardless of Dimitri's handsome, Slavic looks and overly friendly demeanor, Mark instantly hated him, not disliked, but hated him. Mark consciously tried to smile and say hello, but it took all his willpower to suppress the feeling of hatred and be cordial.

Before Mark could answer that they do not do threesomes, Dimitri cut Mark's response off by saying, "I recommend that we all eat at a restaurant I know above the city called Aqua. It is supposed to be the best in town and has a beautiful view of the island."

Indeed, it proved to be the case. The restaurant was excellent and served the best paella Mark had ever eaten. During dinner Eric and Dimitri reminisced about their time in the Special Forces together. Mark was very interested to hear about it since it was a part of Eric's life he never spoke about. Dimitri also reminisced about their treks together up Mount Fitz Roy in Patagonia on the border between Argentina and Chile and Mount Olympus in Greece. Both Eric and Dimitri agreed that mountain climbing changed their view of the world.

Dimitri went out of his way to explain to Mark, "This trek up the volcano at over twelve thousand feet above sea level is much higher than either Mount Fitz Roy at just over ten thousand feet or Mount Olympus at just under ten thousand feet. Therefore, the possibility of altitude sickness and death are much greater, especially since sandstorms, which blow off the Sahara with hundred mile an hour winds can arise within minutes, even on a clear day. And at that height the winds from the Sahara are ice cold, not hot. So, we have to take extra precautions."

Mark knew that Dimitri was trying to get a rise out of him with this information but would not give him the satisfaction. All he said to Dimitri was, "Eric is a big boy, an experienced mountaineer, and quite capable of taking care of himself." Just after this explanation, Mark deliberately reached out and cupped his hand over Eric's on the table in a gesture of possession. He did this without blinking or taking his eyes off Dimitri for a second. Mark realized that, not only was Dimitri very surprised by this, but Dimitri's uncontrolled eye movement gave away Dimitri's real feelings. Dimitri was jealous of Eric and very possibly of Mark's relationship with Eric.

Eric, also surprised, observing this at the table, had the good sense not to move his hand away from Mark and said nothing. But he did think that there was going to be a major fight between him and Mark about him trekking up the mountain with Dimitri when they returned to the villa. Even though Eric and Dimitri continued to heavily drink excellent Spanish wine, Mark switched to club soda for the night. During dinner, Dimitri also boasted many times about the many girlfriends and sex partners he had when he and Eric had been partying together around the world.

So, Mark, to put Dimitri on the spot, finally asked, "Well then, do you consider yourself straight or gay?"

Dimitri responded, "I am buy-sexual. You buy me something and I get sexual." They all laughed at his double meaning response.

But by his response, Mark got another insight into Dimitri, that Dimitri was for sale. When the bill came for dinner and was put on the table, Mark delayed reaching to pay it on purpose. This forced Eric to pay for dinner. Dimitri did not catch it, but by doing this, Eric knew Mark was pissed. Mark also, definitely knew, he was sending a message to Eric.

When they arrived back at the hotel that night, Eric and Dimitri made plans to spend most of the next day together checking gear, permits, and climbing routes on the volcano. They also agreed that depending on the weather and the difficulty of the actual ascent, they had to anticipate the possibility and therefore pack for the possibility, of an overnight stay on the mountain. Even though they would try their hardest to make it only a day trip.

Later in the privacy of their villa at the hotel, Mark said to Eric, "You know that we agreed long ago that you could sleep with anyone you wanted. Because of the difference in our ages, I am fine with that, just as long as you come back to me."

Eric could tell that Mark was gearing up to say more. But before Mark could say anything more, Eric took Mark in his arms, kissed him on his lips, and said, "I don't want anyone else but you."

This went a long way to relaxing Mark. In fact, as usual, Mark emotionally melted in Eric's strong arms. However, the next morning when they made love, Mark's secondary purpose this time was to make sure that Eric was sexually spent before he met Dimitri. Mark trusted Eric, but his gut also told him never to take unnecessary chances, especially with a strikingly handsome, wild man like Dimitri.

As they finished breakfast in their villa, Mark looked Eric straight in the eyes and said, "Eric, I do not trust Dimitri, so be extra careful on the mountain. There is something about him that is not right." Mark did not have the heart to ask Eric not to go since Eric was so excited about going.

Eric knew this was a serious warning from his loving partner, who also had excellent insights about people. So, he therefore answered, "I promise to take your warning very seriously."

The hotel had made available to them a small banquet room where both Eric and Dimitri had the bellmen move their boxed equipment. Eric and Mark walked to the banquet room where Eric planned to meet Dimitri. They quickly hugged good-bye in front of the banquet room entrance. Eric and Dimitri would have the whole day to themselves to prepare for the mountain climbing ascent the next day. Meanwhile, Mark was going to spend it around the pool relaxing.

No sooner had Mark seated himself in a poolside lounge chair with beautiful views of the Atlantic Ocean than he noticed Alisa Reichman, Sam's wife, sitting across the pool.

They waved at each other, and she came over and asked, "Can I join you?"

He responded, "What a nice surprise. I am going to be alone most of the day and am delighted to have the company. But I have to give you a compliment. I have never seen you in a bathing suit before. You have a beautiful figure, very trim, almost muscular."

As she sat down on the lounge chair next to his, Alisa smiled and said, "Thank you. I do a lot of yoga. In fact, I used to teach it years ago and I am planning to take a yoga class this afternoon. I am pretty sure that a beginners' class is being held at the same time at the other end of the pool. Maybe you should try it?"

Mark replied, "It sounds like a plan. I have never tried yoga before, but it looks easy."

Alisa's understated response was, "Well, do as much as you can and don't overdo it."

Next, he asked, "Is Sam here too?"

Alisa's short, calm reply was, "I think he's floating around somewhere close by. He should be here soon."

Mark noted that, "Well, I feel better now. I felt a little naked without Sam here to protect us." Alisa just smiled and nodded her head in agreement. As Alisa intended, Mark was unaware of what was happening or who he was really talking too.

As they settled in, to relax, he could not help but ask her, "Do you know a Dimitri Sokolov, a former member of the Israeli Special Forces and Eric's team partner for their ascent on the volcano tomorrow? And if so, what is your opinion of him?"

Alisa's very careful answer, almost as if she expected the question, worried Mark even more. She said, "Yes, I know of him. He had a reputation as an excellent soldier but was passed over for promotion and quit the military because of it. Later, I heard, he became a well paid mercenary and a professional mountain climbing guide. I know Eric and Dimitri have been friends for years. Eric stuck by his friend Dimitri through all of it."

Mark guessed there was a lot more to the story, but he would not discover the rest today. They continued their poolside chat with Mark asking about her kids.

She replied, "They are all fine. My eldest son, David, just got engaged so maybe Sam and I will be grandparents one of these days. My second son, Boaz, is about to enter engineering school and my youngest, Micah, just finished his first year at university with excellent grades." She then started to read her a novel she had brought with her, signaling to Mark to relax and enjoy the day.

Mark tried to relax, lying back on his lounge chair but still felt unsettled. He tried to analyze why he felt this way. He knew Eric could take care of himself under almost all situations even with someone like Dimitri. As he drifted off to sleep, feeling the gentle, balmy breezes from Africa caressing him, he finally connected the dots.

He immediately sat straight up, startling Alisa whose lounge chair was next to his. He had just deduced what was bothering him. It was Dimitri's use of the phrase "large endowment." It was a very polite way of saying big cock or big dick and was out of character for a man like Dimitri to use. So, Mark thought, *Just where have I heard that phrase before?* He remembered that Eric had used it when Eric was describing what the assistant director of Mossad, Gideon Avraham, had said when he offered him the honeypot assignment. Mark asked himself, *Is there a connection between Dimitri and Gideon?* But he also thought that his thinking might be too conspiratorial or perhaps clouded by jealousy of Dimitri. After all, Dimitri and Eric were longtime friends, both the same age, both extremely handsome and shared the love of mountain climbing together.

All this went through Mark's mind in a flash. He then just turned to Alisa and said, "Sorry to scare you but I just developed a hunch."

Alisa, for an instant, dropped her warm wife/family persona facade and stared back at him, revealing the cold icy stare of a lethal Mossad agent analyzing the situation. But she quickly balanced herself and returned to a much more friendly stare and tone when she asked, "Are you all right?"

Mark replied, "Never better."

When Eric entered the hotel banquet room, Dimitri was already there. He looked refreshed and ready for the day with a good night's sleep. Eric's initial morning impression of his friend was that Dimitri can certainly hold his liquor.

The first thing Dimitri said to Eric was not good morning but, "Your friend Mark hates me."

Eric didn't try to deny it, simply responding, "A lot of people have that reaction to you."

As they spread their equipment on four banquet tables, laid out in two separate sections with two tables end to end in each section, Dimitri, without looking at Eric while they were unloading and arranging their equipment on the tables, asked Eric, "So, do you love Mark?"

Eric succinctly replied, "I married him."

Dimitri knew his reply meant "yes." However, Dimitri pressed the point by saying, "I didn't know you swung that way, or we both could have had a whack at it. It would have been fun. Remember that time in Santiago when we were both horny and couldn't find any girls? Together we would be unstoppable and write our own ticket for the future."

Eric put down the piece of equipment he was holding, turned to look directly at Dimitri, and said, "I think that would be a disaster on many levels. You know I like you as a good friend. Let's keep it that way."

All Dimitri said in response was, "Eric, you are always full of surprises."

Eric was also very well aware that his longtime friend did not take rejection well. Thus, he realized that this was yet another reason to be extra careful on their ascent together.

After that, everything was about their preparation for their trek the next day. First, they continued to inspect and count all their equipment. Eric reviewed and tested every piece of equipment twice. They knew their lives would depend on it when on the volcano. They also reviewed all the geographical maps and preferred trekking routes up Mount Tiede as well the permits given them by the Spanish government to take a special route for their ascent on the volcano. Since they had to anticipate spending the night at over twelve thousand feet above sea level, they had to also carry a tent, sleeping bag pods, and a small stove. This was in addition to rope, crampons (which look like steel claws or spikes attached to their boots), for piercing ice and snow, climbing harnesses, ice axes and ice screws (to be hammered into the ice), lightweight pulleys, carabiners (metal rings), helmets, goggles, one collapsable ladder to traverse ice crevasses or rock fissures, additional cord for making slings in case of a fall, and last a lightweight backpack to store it all. The navigational tools for the ascent included an altimeter watch for each climber, a personal location beacon, GPS, and maps. The miracle of all this was that if it was packed correctly, it could all be stored in two backpacks with the total load weighing fifty pounds each. Finally, in addition to the backpack, there was a 1.5 liter hydration system carried on a climber's belt so that a climber can drink at will and a mobile oxygen face mask worn over the nose and mouth that could make its own oxygen and equalize outside pressure to relieve breathing resistance at high altitudes. And, of course, they packed suntan lotion. The sun at those high altitudes was beastly strong.

The backpacks took all day to pack. Both Dimitri and Eric skipped lunch to make sure everything was ready for the climb the next morning. They were both ravenous by dinner time. Both had their strict protocols for the night before a climb. Dimitri ate alone and drank no alcohol. He needed to focus his mind. Eric ate with Mark at the hotel and also drank no alcohol. Mark could tell that Eric was almost completely focused on the next day. However, Mark did bring up his theory on the possibility of Dimitri's connection with Gideon Avraham.

But Eric just told him, "You are too paranoid, just relax." Actually, Eric tensed inwardly without showing Mark. He silently thought to himself that Mark's keen observation was correct. But he did not want Mark to worry.

However, during dinner, Mark couldn't help himself when he asked this one question. He had studied the diagrams of how the climbing harness fit over the exterior, insulated climbing suit. So, he wondered, "Eric, how are you going to urinate when wearing your climbing harness over your climbing suit?"

Eric simply answered, "Mountain climbers don't take it off to pee. We just pee inside it. The temperature is usually so cold that the pee freezes almost instantly."

Mark braced himself to show no emotion when Eric said this—matching Eric's nonchalance about it. But inside, Mark sarcastically thought, *This mountain-climbing trek just keeps getting better and better!* Also at this time, he made a promise to himself that this was the last mountain he was going to let the love of his life climb! Outwardly, all Mark did was give Eric a slight smile to acknowledge Eric's answer.

Since Eric knew that Mark would be very altitude sensitive, he next asked Mark to stay at the hotel and not come to the viewing and tourist rest area near the lower base of the cable car at approximately three thousand feet high. Eric downplayed the views, saying, "You won't be able to see much from the lower base anyway. Our real trek starts at the end of the cable ride more than eight thousand feet high. But there is a real possibility of severe altitude sickness at the lower rest area base as well if you are not acclimated."

Mark reluctantly agreed although he knew he would be okay even at over five thousand feet above sea level based on his business trips to Denver, Colorado years ago. Nevertheless, he acquiesced to Eric's wishes. Mark understood Eric's well meaning but firm real message that he was not wanted on any part of this trek.

Eric finished by saying, "I need to get up at 4:00 a.m. tomorrow to catch the van to the base of the cable car ride on the volcano, and I am really so excited about climbing the last half mile to the rim. You know, it's covered in ice and snow and will be especially challenging. But I am also looking forward to taking photos on the rim of the caldera and seeing the rivers of molten lava below. I promise to film everything for you." Lastly, he cautioned Mark, "If all goes well, there is a strong possibility we can do the whole trek in one day and won't spend the night. However, it depends on many factors, including the changeable weather and toughness of the terrain."

Neither Mark nor Eric could sleep that night. This was due to Mark's dread of the danger facing his partner the next day and Eric's adrenaline filled anticipation of an exciting and challenging climb. Mark tried to analyze his feelings. They weren't just the dangers of the climb, but it was something about Dimitri he still could not put his finger on.

The next morning was hectic. Mark tried to help when he offered to carry some of their equipment, but the two mountaineers had strict procedures of who could or could not touch it before an ascent. So, while Eric and Dimitri carried

their own gear, Mark helped by holding doors open from the banquet room through the hotel to the waiting van and driver. They quickly loaded the van and drove away. As Mark watched the van leave, as he stood all alone in the darkness before the dawn, he could not shake the feeling of danger to his partner.

All of a sudden after about ten feet, the van jerked to a stop. Eric had shouted to the van driver to stop, saying, "I've forgotten something." Eric jumped out of the van, ran back to Mark, grabbed him, and gave him a huge hug and kiss, saying, "Just remember that I'm your lover as well as your partner and I will be back soon to prove it. Go get some breakfast. I will call you from the top of the volcano when I get there." Not giving Mark a chance to respond, he turned and ran back to the van, jumped in, and the van sped away.

Mark returned to their villa, showered and went down to the restaurant, thinking he would be the first one there. He was mistaken. Alisa Reichman was already seated and waving at him to join her for breakfast.

The van arrived at the cable car base just as dawn was breaking. It took them only a few minutes to load their gear on to the cable car that was built to hold forty people. The cable car ride itself only took about ten minutes. Moreover, at this hour, they were all by themselves. During the ride they had extraordinary views of the sunrise over the entire island of Tenerife and distant Gran Canaria Island. Also, from the cable car ride as they passed above it, they were able to look down at the very impressive astrological observatory located high on the volcano. When they arrived at the end, they took a few minutes to gear up. Dimitri graciously volunteered to carry their only expandable aluminum ladder.

But instead of hiking to the rim of the volcano via the tourist path, they first trekked more than 1,500 feet down and around the outside of the crater for more than three miles to get to the base of the almost vertical north face. Eric took videos as they passed through landscapes that he thought looked like Mars—barren, windswept sandy slopes at an almost forty-five degree angle, interspersed with towering, vertical lava pillars, grotesquely shaped from eruptions millions of years ago. As they looked up at the half mile high wall of snow and ice to the caldera's rim, they noticed the now constant wind had turned very cold. To be on the safe side, they both decided to wear their oxygen masks going forward.

After observing this ascent area firsthand, Dimitri turned to Eric and said, "We have to be extremely careful where we hammer our ice screws holding our ropes because I noticed the fierce winds here have packed the rock fissures with loose snow, no good to hold an ice screw." They tossed a coin who would lead. Dimitri won and would ascend the volcano's sheer north face with Eric following. Both were bound together with climbing rope hooked on lightweight but incredibly strong metal rings for safety. Both were depending on each other. One false move and one could fall to his death, dragging the other with him. Eric asked Dimitri if he wanted him to take his turn carrying the ladder. But Dimitri said he was still fine carrying the extra weight of their expandable ladder. To relieve the tension Dimitri joked, "You get to look at my perfect ass all the way to the rim of the mountain."

Eric replied, "This is the one tragedy of this ascent that I have to look up at your flabby ass, all the way up. Go to a gym once in a while and tighten it up! Maybe if you did, you could get yourself a wife or a husband." This friendly locker room banter continued all the way up the ascent.

Luckily, both were advanced level mountain climbers in perfect physical shape and climbed like mountain goats once they started. They found that they were climbing on about two feet thick of ice covered with a layer of snow, all on top of a lava rock surface. It was perfect to hold the ice screws. At almost 12,000 feet, a hidden lava rock fissure opened up all the way to the top rim. The pounding of their ice axes to hammer their ice screws into the layer of ice covering it caused the ice and snow to shake loose from it. Both Eric and Dimitri noticed that once the fissure started to become visible, the ice and snow continued to fall away, revealing a two mile drop to the bottom, with the distinct possibility that if someone fell into it, the body would never be found. Laughing at their near miss, Dimitri proposed that by pressing their boots on one side of the smooth, almost glass-like, fissure wall and their backpacks pressed against the other equally smooth wall, they could horizontally walk to the top of the fissure to get to the rim. Eric had done this advanced climbing maneuver several times before and immediately agreed.

But as he agreed, he suddenly realized that Dimitri had nothing to lose if Dimitri died doing this. Whereas he would lose Mark, the love of his life. He realized he had something for which to live. He asked himself, as he braced against the opposite lava rock fissure walls, *Is the major adrenaline rush I'm having worth it?* For the first time in his life, he doubted if it was. It was at this moment he promised himself that this would be his last mountain climbing adventure.

They both continued slowly but horizontally walking up the sides of the fissure, the rest of the way to the rim of the caldera. When they arrived at the top, they untethered themselves from each other and took off their backpacks as they stood on the rim, marveling at the spectacular views in the brilliant midday sunlight. In fact, the sunlight was so strong and brilliant at the top that they were both very glad they were wearing dark sunglasses and plenty of protective sunscreen. Eric and Dimitri were in excellent spirits having conquered another mountain. They both took photos of themselves together and alone as they stood on the rim of the volcano's crater with awe inspiring views in the background. Eric, however, thought the most dramatic photos were the multicolored rocks on the floor of the volcano's crater surrounded by sheer cliffs. He knew that the yellowish color on some of the lava rocks was pure sulfur. He could actually see streams of red hot molten lava meandering through the older solidified rocks protruding from the floor of the crater. While standing on the crater's narrow rim, they could also smell the poisonous sulfur gas drifting up from deep in the earth below. The gas had a yellowish color, smelled like rotten eggs and engulfed them. Surprisingly, this heightened the feeling of pride of accomplishment in both men alongside the feeling of danger.

Dimitri turned to Eric and said, "I am surprised that even at this height the smell of sulfur dioxide is so strong." Looking at the whole island below them and the horizon beyond, like being on top of the world, gave both men a huge adrenaline rush.

Eric tried calling Mark to tell him he had reached the summit early and would not have to spend the night but got no answer. So, he left a message. About twenty minutes later, Eric said to Dimitri, "If we want to get off the volcano before it gets dark, it's time to make a decision about the way back down. There are two choices for the way down. First, we could return by climbing down the way we came. Or secondly, we could walk along the rim for about two miles to the side of the volcano from which the tourists approach and then take a relatively easy hike down to the cable car pick up point. The second is the easier route except that the fissure we just climbed cuts across our way back."

Dimitri instantly said, "Luckily, we brought an expandable ladder that can traverse the top of the space. Let's take the easy way back."

Eric was surprised to hear Dimitri wanted to take the easy way. He thought it was way out of character for him. But Eric agreed. They both geared up for the trek by reattaching the climbing ropes but did not yet put their backpacks on. The first one across the fissure would catch the cumbersome backpacks the other one would throw across to him so they could both walk across without the extra weight and with better balance.

Dimitri quickly took the lightweight, almost indestructible aluminum ladder attached to his backpack, opened it to the length needed to overlap the edges on either side of the fissure, and laid it across the top of it. After pushing the ends of the ladder into the snow to firm its position across the chasm below, Dimitri walked out to the middle of the ladder, both feet on its outside edges, and then abruptly reversed himself by jumping and turning around in midair at the same time and walked back. Smiling, he told Eric, "I was just testing it."

Eric did not like that escapade by Dimitri. Since they had just reattached themselves to the climbing ropes for safety, he told Dimitri, "You could have killed us both if you had fallen."

Dimitri just smiled, ignoring Eric's comment. Eric then knelt down and hammered in one of their ice screws on this side. He then pulled the climbing rope into the metal ring attached to it and knotted it before either of them crossed again. Dimitri then proceeded to easily walk all the way across the ladder this time. What Eric did not notice was that Dimitri, after starting by walking on the ladder rungs, switched to using only the outside edges of the ladder midway across. When Dimitri got to the other side, Eric threw both backpacks across for Dimitri to catch. By luck, instinct, or professionalism, Eric now insisted that Dimitri hammer in the ice screw on Dimitri's side and proceed to tie off their climbing rope while Eric watched him do it.

Dimitri certainly complied but loudly said to Eric, "You are such a pussy for not immediately following me across without needing any of these extra precautions."

As soon as Eric saw Dimitri finish knotting the rope through the ring on the newly hammered ice screw, Eric started cautiously walking across on the ladder's rungs. He was looking directly at Dimitri and not looking down. When he was about midpoint on the ladder, he noticed that Dimitri's eyes seemed overly anxious. In fact, he noticed Dimitri's whole body seemed very tense and anxious. He thought that maybe his old friend Dimitri was really worried about him crossing safely. But he soon discovered it wasn't his safety that made Dimitri anxious. As Eric put his full weight on the middle rung of the ladder and was about to step on another, the rung gave way, causing Eric to fall headfirst off the ladder. As he fell, Eric was able to grab the next rung of the ladder to try to halt his fall. As his powerful hand grasped the next rung, it also gave way.

He fell almost fifteen feet before his climbing rope and harness abruptly caught his waist mid-fall. Had it been a longer fall before the rope and harness stopped it, his increased speed and weight falling would have broken his back in two as he hung horizontally suspended in midair. Additionally, his sun goggles were jerked off his head when he abruptly stopped falling, shattering into dozens of pieces against the lava rock walls. Eric instinctively grabbed the climbing cord attached to his harness that was saving his life and pulled it. This reflexive pulling motion straightened his hanging body to a vertical position held by his harness. He had the wind knocked out of him for a moment but caught his breath and started to review his precarious situation. He noted that the angle of the rope had swung his body around so that he was now hanging directly over the caldera with its sheer walls and not inside the fissure. This meant he would not be able to walk himself up the fissure walls like before.

Eric could also hear Dimitri's voice calling his name asking if he was all right. But he could not see Dimitri from his hanging position. There was no question in his mind that the ladder rungs had been cut. He sadly realized that this was no accident but a deliberate murder attempt by his friend! He yelled up to Dimitri that he was a little out of breath but fine.

Dimitri's answer was most revealing. Dimitri walked to the edge of the fissure so they now could also see one another. He then yelled down to Eric, "You are sure hard to kill— just like me!"

Eric yelled back one word, "Why?"

That's when Dimitri replied by berating Eric, "You're so pretty but so stupid not to read what is happening."

Eric yelled back, "You don't want to know what I did to the last man who said that to me."

Dimitri just sneered and said, "I went back to the hotel banquet room at night and cut the ladder rungs myself after you had checked them earlier." He continued, "There is a military coup in Israel happening as we speak. Gideon Avraham is taking over the government with the help of four brigadier generals from the High Command. And he is eliminating all supporters of the incompetent, democratically elected Knesset and any potential competition or distractions to his new government. That includes you because of your popularity in Israel. Then we will eliminate your boyfriend, Mark. I was instructed to do it in that order because we couldn't leave a vengeful hunter-killer like yourself alive if we killed Mark first and missed you. We will announce you had a fatal mountain climbing accident, and Mark had a heart attack when he heard the news—nice and neat."

Eric then asked, "But what do you get from this besides the money they obviously paid you?"

Dimitri cooly responded, "I am being reinstated with the rank of colonel into the Israeli Defense Force." He added, "Everyone opposed to us will be declared traitors to Israel!"

Eric yelled back, "Dimitri, you and your co-conspirators are the real traitors to Israel and democracy!"

Dimitri laughed and replied, "Only if we lose. If we win, we are patriots!"

Eric could not permit Dimitri to have the last word as he shouted back to Dimitri, "You have no loyalty to anyone or anything but yourself. You will also betray your new government if it benefits you!"

Next, Dimitri took out his cell phone, turned away from Eric so he couldn't hear, and dialed his contact in the hotel, saying, "It's time. Kill Mark now."

But Eric overheard this call. Sound travels very clearly in the stillness of the clear high altitude air. When he heard Dimitri order Mark's death, any remaining feelings of loyalty to his old friend evaporated. Almost simultaneously, Eric pressed a hidden button on the inside of his collar three times without Dimitri noticing.

Dimitri then turned back to give Eric his full attention. Dimitri continued, "I have a choice to make now. I can leave you hanging here and let nature gradually kill you. But I think not. With your instincts and survival skills you might survive that. So, I think I have the solution." He then took out an automatic switch blade, pressed a small button on its side, releasing a dagger knife capable of cutting the rope on which Eric's life depended. Eric clearly saw what he intended to do.

Dimitri added, "If you somehow survive the fall, the molten lava or poisonous sulfur fumes should get you."

Eric yelled back, "Just out of curiosity, I have one last request. Could you tell me who issued the kill order on me and Mark and also who hired you and who will you report to?"

Dimitri, looking down at Eric helplessly hanging in midair, replied, "Well, given the circumstances, I guess it won't hurt for you to know this. It's the least I can do for an old friend. Gideon Avraham personally issued the kill order on you and Mark. I will report to Brigadier General Lev Vakim, who is currently rounding up in a surprise raid all members of the Knesset and military officers who oppose us. Also, for the record the prime minister and the director of Mossad know nothing about the coup. But they will be court-martialed and either executed or put in prison for life."

Eric yelled back, "You and the others are nothing but traitors to Israel. Consider us no longer friends. And as far as who is the stupid one, this was a trap which you fell right into! Now turn around!"

Surprised by Eric's commanding tone in his precarious situation, Dimitri turned around, still holding his opened switch blade knife, to face *Dragon Fire*, the aerial battleship, floating silently behind him. The last thing Dimitri saw through its clear glass front windows were the two pilots, Gil

Sofer and Elon Dagen, with Colonel Sam Reichman standing behind them. Dimitri also thought he could read Colonel Reichman's lips as the colonel said, "By my command" Then a blinding laser light appeared for a moment and poof—Dimitri Sokolov did not exist any longer—just a little black cloud of smoke remained where he had stood.

Colonel Sam Reichman then ordered *Dragon Fire* to pivot around so its side door aligned directly against the dangling Eric Jansen. He also had the pilots and himself put on oxygen masks before they opened the door and let the pressurized air escape to prevent fainting due to the quick change in oxygen levels at more than 12,000 feet above sea level.

The senior pilot, Gil Sofer, mentioned to Sam Reichman that the new anti-gravity engine should theoretically compensate for the difference in air pressure at this height when they opened the side door to retrieve Colonel Jansen. However, it had never been done before. So, he was interested to test it. "The worst that could happen is that we crash onto the volcano floor," he said, smiling.

Sam Reichman winced when he heard this but still ordered the door opened. Hanging out the door himself, he then used his considerable strength to grab his friend Colonel Eric Jansen and pulled him safely into the aircraft. Now it was Sam's turn to smile at his trussed-up friend when he said, "Did you enjoy hanging around on your vacation?" He started to laugh at his own joke.

Eric thanked his friend for saving his life but thought Sam's joke was clever but not particularly funny. So he ignored it, while quickly saying, "I am very worried that Mark is in mortal danger and we need to get back to the hotel to prevent any harm coming to him."

Sam calmly replied, "We are on our way, but you don't have to worry. The Viper is protecting him."

Eric was relieved to hear this because he knew that the Viper was one of Mossad's deadliest and most effective agents. He then called Mark's cell phone but got no answer again. So, he left a message, saying, "Mark, you are in danger of being assassinated. Go to the villa, lock the doors and wait for me. I am on my way." Eric then unhitched himself from his climbing harness as they maneuvered the aircraft closely above the volcano's rim, allowing him to jump out to gather all their gear and throw it into the aircraft so as to leave no trace of their ascent. After this, *Dragon Fire* sped off to the hotel. From the volcano's peak, they arrived in less than ten minutes on the isolated lava field just beyond the landscaped part of their hotel, close to the villa where Eric and Mark were staying.

While traveling on *Dragon Fire*, Sam and Eric exchanged information about what was occurring in Israel. First, Eric gave Sam the information he'd received from Dimitri about the coup, saying, "Dimitri told me that four brigadier generals are part of the coup, and that at this moment Brigadier General Lev Vakim is arresting all the Knesset members and military officers that oppose them. That Gideon Avraham is the ringleader. But that the prime minister and the director of Mossad are not part of the coup."

Sam replied, "Thank God, Gideon's timing was off. Jacob moved forcibly against the coup members early this morning before they had time to strike. Gideon Avraham has already been arrested. However, your new information helps to confirm Gideon Avraham's guilt. But it's news to me that Lev Vakim is part of this coup. Jacob is directing all measures against the traitors so let me call him now. Lev Vakim will be arrested immediately if Jacob hasn't already done so." With that Sam called Jacob to update each other.

After the call, Sam turned to Eric and said, "I want to inform you that Jacob has successfully moved against the conspirators but warn you that only a few of us know that there was an attempted coup. So it's top secret that it took place. Also I want to tell you that Lt. Colonel Stein has signed off on your PTSD therapy closure and those records have been sealed. Additionally, both Jacob and I want to deeply thank you for putting yourself and Mark in danger for the sake of democracy in Israel, using yourself and Mark as bait to flush out members of the coup!"

Eric humbly replied, "I am very thankful to Jacob for taking me into his confidence at the party, alerting me as to what was about to happen and asking me to help stop it."

Sam continued, "Let me further update you. Jacob has forced the prime minister to resign and call for early new elections. The PM has already announced his resignation was due to health reasons. The president of the Knesset is acting PM until the new election. The director of the Mossad has also been forced to resign, saying it was for personal reasons."

Eric seemed puzzled by these resignations. So, Sam explained, while looking at Eric straight in the eyes. "Stupidity governing is equally as bad as culpability in something as important as a military coup."

Next, Eric asked Sam, "Well, since both directors are gone, who will debrief me?"

Sam calmly answered, "You were just debriefed. I am the new director of the Mossad." Eric was both surprised but glad at the same time by his friend's answer. Sam added, "Jacob wants us both to return to Israel as soon as possible in case we're needed. However, we believe our actions here were the last nail in the coup's coffin."

Back at the hotel, Mark had decided to spend another lazy day around the pool after having breakfast with Alisa. She excused herself and disappeared after breakfast, mumbling that she had something to do.

Mark thought, *I can never keep track of her. She moves so quickly from place to place.* As he walked back to his villa to change into his bathing suit, he could tell that it was going to be another beautiful, balmy day by the pool. However, his anxiety over the danger that Eric faced climbing that damn volcano, mixed with the boredom he was now feeling, made him want to leave this place as soon as possible. While walking to his pool lounge chair, he happened to walk past an extremely handsome, dark haired, brown eyed man who caught his eye. Mark observed that the young man was in his late twenties, six foot tall and wearing fitted blue jeans without a belt that seemed to hang around his waist by itself with a white linen shirt unbuttoned almost all the way to his navel, revealing perfectly cut abs with his sleeves rolled up to the middle part of his forearm. His white linen shirt sleeves couldn't roll up any further because the young man's muscles were too big. All this was set against a beautiful dark tan, brilliant white smile and dark brown bedroom eyes. In other words, Mark thought the guy was gorgeous by any standards.

Mark couldn't believe it when he looked back for a moment and the guy winked at him and smiled.

Instantly Mark was wide awake and feeling better. He immediately stopped, turned, walked back, and introduced himself to this Mediterranean hunk. His name was Alejandro, and he was the hotel's new masseur, but he doubled as a pool attendant when he was not busy. He had just flown in from Madrid yesterday. Mark was very flattered that someone so handsome and friendly had winked at him. He had not flirted in years with a handsome stranger. Mark could not help but notice Alejandro's white linen shirt fluttering against his hard body as they spoke. Of course, he booked a one hour massage that day for early afternoon with Alejandro. He thought, *What a sexy distraction.* In fact, he was so distracted that he forgot he had left his cell phone in the room.

Staying all day by the pool, watching Alejandro work serving drinks and delivering towels, he was right on time for his 2:00 p.m. massage with Alejandro. Mark didn't bother with the steam room. He just took a quick shower and lay flat on the massage table with a towel covering his rear. Alejandro was an excellent masseur. At the beginning of the massage, before Mark became too relaxed to talk, he had a short conversation with Alejandro and discovered that his masseur was not Spanish but Israeli descended from Spanish Jews. He thought this fact was interesting but nothing special since the hotel was Israeli owned. Mark also could not help but notice that Alejandro massaged him with his shirt off, revealing a tanned, well-muscled upper torso, which Mark thought was a very sexy.

During the massage Alejandro excused himself to take a very short cell phone call while Mark was still lying face down. He then returned to continue the massage. This did not interfere with Mark's total relaxation at all. About five minutes later, Alejandro said he needed to go into the other room to get some special massage oil. But this time Mark noticed there was a long minute before he returned. He also thought he heard a muffled scuffling sound. Suddenly, Alejandro's naked upper body slumped across Mark's back as he was still lying face down on the table.

Mark was shocked by this, turning immediately to sit up, feeling Alejandro's still warm body slide against his to the floor. His eyes focused on a small drop of blood on the back of Alejandro's neck. He quickly realized that Alisa, aka the Viper, was standing in front of him with her left hand on her slightly askew hips, while holding up an empty syringe with attached hypodermic needle in her right hand. She casually held it like she was holding a cigarette.

Smiling, all she said to tease him and lighten the mood was, "A good six pack of abs will do it every time!"

He was nonplussed, speechless, almost in shock, looking at Alejandro's obviously dead body on the floor. However, he did manage to say, "Alisa, I swear nothing happened. I was only getting a massage."

She replied, "Don't be so guilty. I know that. I have been watching you both." She saw Mark focus at what she was holding. So, she moved her hand with the hypodermic needle and empty syringe closer to Mark giving him a good look. She then simply said, "This was meant for you. But I stuck him with it instead. It contained liquid cyanide poison. It would have looked like you died of a heart attack. It works almost instantly, and no one would have found the little puncture wound at the base of the back of your neck."

All Mark could say was to ask, "Are you sure?"

Alisa replied, "I'm sure. Cyanide smells like bitter almonds. Want to smell the syringe?"

Mark shook his head to indicate definitely "No."

Alisa continued, "The masseur had to have major help to use a sophisticated poison like this. Not the kind of thing an amateur like him could have put together by himself. I know who helped him and have already taken care of them. And for the record, the masseur is not Israeli but a hired killer from Sicily. I had to let this play out to make sure I got all of them." She then said, "Well, it's time for you to get dressed and for us to get back to your villa. Do you ever answer your phone? Eric has been calling you."

Mark only then realized he didn't have his phone and must have left it in the room. He felt like an idiot.

Alisa continued, "I will step out for a minute for you to get dressed. Then I will brief you on the way."

Before Alisa left, Mark sincerely thanked her for saving his life.

All Alisa said in response was, "You're welcome."

Mark hurriedly dressed and was ready to leave in less than three minutes.

As they walked Mark's first question was to ask about Eric.

Alisa replied, "Sam is with Eric, and they are both fine. In fact, they are on their way here now. Therefore, we have to hurry back to the villa with just a quick stop in my room to pick up my bag." However, she did not mention anything about Dimitri. She continued, "Pack all your bags and be ready to leave as soon as they get back."

Mark, getting his bearings while walking, asked her, "What about the dead body we left on floor of the spa?"

Alisa just replied, "What part of—the hotel is managed by Mossad—don't you understand? Meaning everything will be removed and scrubbed."

Mark now added one more important question, "But why did he try to kill me?"

Alisa replied, "My best guess is that someone in Israel does not like your high profile gay marriage and Eric's growing political popularity."

Mark understood immediately that he was only getting a partial answer but accepted it for now.

Once in the villa, he heard his cell phone beeping and saw the many messages from Eric. Again, he felt stupid. He packed their bags quickly and waited for Eric and Sam to arrive. In the meantime, Mark read and listened to all the messages from Eric and saw all the photos and videos of his mountain climbing trek. He also shared them with Alisa. They both agreed that Eric and Dimitri looked like they were safe and having a great time.

Just a few minutes later, Eric and Sam rushed into the room. Eric and Mark immediately embraced each other, holding each other so tight they could hardly breath, while kissing each other hard on the lips. Mark then pointed to Alisa and said to Eric, "Alisa saved my life!"

Eric nodded at her and said, "Thank you from the bottom of my heart."

Next Sam stepped forward to give his wife of over thirty years a kiss on the cheek and said, "Thank you, honey."

She just replied, "You're welcome, sweetie."

Sam then handed Mark a document and said, "Please sign this. It is an NDA, a non-disclosure agreement. You have to sign it because you are about to experience something that most people still don't know exist, let alone fly in, and you cannot tell anybody or you will go to prison. Everyone here has signed it, including Eric, and it also covers anything else the Israeli government considers top secret."

Mark took a hotel pen from a table and without reading it, signed it. Sam folded the signed document and put it in his pocket. He added, "Eric will explain in more detail to you what you just signed at another time. We now have to hurry and leave."

Mark replied, "Wait a minute, I hate saying this. Eric, I love you, but you stink! So, I think we need to give you fifteen minutes to shower and change clothes. I insist."

Eric took the hint, saying, "It's the sulfur gas from the volcano you smell. It smells like rotten eggs and has permeated my clothes and hair." He turned, took some new clothes from his luggage and sprinted to the bathroom while stripping off his old clothes. The last thing they all saw was his nude backside just before he slammed the bathroom door behind him.

Alisa commented, "He's got a great pair of buns. But you should have seen Sam when we met. He had a body like Hercules and buns of steel." With that, she patted her husband on his backside and said, "They are still hard as steel!"

Mark saw Sam actually blush while giving a big smile to his wife for the compliment. Alisa added, "Luckily after I married him, he decided to stop playing ice hockey in Canada before he lost any teeth. He still has such a beautiful smile."

Embarrassed, Sam tried to stop smiling so he could hide his teeth because he knew Mark and Alisa were focusing on them. It was apparent to Mark that these two were still very much in love after decades of marriage.

Eric came zooming out of the bathroom, all clean and ready to travel. Alisa said the hotel staff would box and send anything left behind. So, they grabbed their bags and walked away from the hotel with its lush landscaping and on to the barren, jagged lava rock fields beyond. Sitting on top of the lava was something that looked to Mark like a spaceship. Mark realized as he approached that this aircraft was not actually sitting on anything. It was just floating silently in the air about half a foot above the lava with its shiny silver skin reflecting the sunlight. As they approached the door of the aircraft, it slid open, revealing what Mark thought was a very high tech interior. It was an easy step up to get in. He realized that this must be *Dragon Fire*, the aerial battleship he had heard about and had saved Eric and his fellow commandos in Africa.

Mark really didn't know or understand what he was looking at inside. He was impressed however, when the senior pilot, Captain Gil Sofer, told everyone to strap in and they would arrive in Israel in one hour and fifteen minutes.

Mark said loudly, "It's impossible to get back so fast from this distance."

The copilot, Elon Dagen, yelled back to Mark, "Not when we are going Mach 3—three times the speed of sound. So just sit back and enjoy the awesome views."

Mark, leaning forward in his seat, yelled back to the pilots, "Okay then. We're all ready. So, PUNCH IT!" Mark turned to everyone and said, "I always wanted to say that."

They all laughed as *Dragon Fire* headed vertically straight up above the clouds and streaked away. During the flight Mark questioned Sam about not feeling any atmospheric pressure due to the change in elevation and speed.

All Sam said in response was, "Yes, you are correct."

They all admired Mark but thought the less Mark knew the better.

Mark understood everything about this trip was top secret. So, he decided to change the subject and ask Eric about Dimitri. He said the photos Eric had sent him from the rim of the volcano were extraordinary and showed they were both having a great time. Mark took a deep breath before he asked Eric, "By the way, are you planning on seeing Dimitri again soon?"

Eric turned to Mark and answered, "Dimitri is no longer a friend of mine, and no, I am not planning on seeing him again. And I can't tell you anymore."

Mark was a little surprised but relieved at Eric's response as he replied, "Fine with me. I don't trust the guy."

While they all settled in for the trip back to Israel, Jacob Kurtz phoned Eric. The pilots were able to transfer the call through their comm link. He started by saying, "Everything is under control in Israel, and I want to personally thank you for successfully using yourself and Mark as bait in helping prevent the coup. I also want to talk to you about something important when you return."

Eric replied, "Can't you tell me now?"

There was a short silence on the phone. Then, Jacob said, "We want you to run for prime minister of Israel. It's your time. Think about it." With that said, Jacob abruptly hung up, as was his style.

Eric was surprised and excited at what Jacob had just said. However, he wanted Mark's approval before deciding. Eric inwardly knew that he needed Mark by his side to keep himself in balance and his dark side safely tucked away, especially if he was elected to such a powerful position. He looked across to where Sam was sitting facing him. Sam had a knowing smile on his face. Eric guessed that Sam already knew what Jacob had just asked him on the phone. He then turned to Mark and asked, "How would you like to be the First Gentleman of Israel? They want me to run for PM. Is it okay with you? I am sure it will be a tough election. I can't do it without you."

Mark was also surprised but not overwhelmed. He thought Eric would have an incredible political career ahead of him if Eric decided he wanted it. So, knowing this was a rare negotiable moment between them, Mark asked, "Will you promise me that your mountain climbing days are over if I agree?"

Eric immediately said, "I already made the decision climbing the volcano that this would be my last mountain climbing expedition. Basically, because I don't want you to worry about me."

Mark warmly replied, "Then I agree. Let's do it. Sounds like a great adventure."

Strapped into their seats side by side, they couldn't hug to seal the promise, so they just held each other's hand. Both of them were so excited about Eric's future political career.

However, as Eric leaned back into his seat, he thought, *There is no way in hell I am ever telling Mark that I allowed the Mossad to use us as bait, putting us both in mortal danger to hunt and kill those coup conspirators. I'd rather be dangling on that rope on top of the volcano again than have that conversation!*

ABOUT THE AUTHOR

Mark Akst is retired and lives in Fort Lauderdale, Florida. *The Mossad Warrior Spy* is his third novel in a series. His professional career included managing hotels in several US cities. He has travelled extensively in North America, Europe and the Middle East. His passionate hobbies are archeology and history. He has a Bachelor of Arts degree from the University of Pennsylvania and an MBA from New York University. All his novels were written for his readers as a fun escape in a stressful world. Visit him at markakst.com